Jake's Heart

ADORA ROSE

WARRU PRESS

This book is dedicated to my late neighbour Rose Heath, who let me borrow her books in her wardrobe and introduced me to the world of romance. To one of the most caring, thoughtful and fun people. You are remembered.

I acknowledge the Noongar Whadjuk people, the first story tellers of the land on which this book is written. I pay respect to the elders and storytellers: past, present and emerging.

Chapter One

Students gathered in the corridor of Ocean Bay High School on Monday morning, excitedly greeting each other as though they hadn't been spending their summer with their friends. Brian Vance, the star football player, walked through the entrance and students would stop talking to get out of the way, clearing a path for him to walk down the hall. Brian reached his locker where his friends Eric, Lamont, and William waited.

"It's about time you showed up." Eric patted Brian on the back. "Thought you were skipping today."

"And not tell you guys that we could hang out? That would never happen," Brian laughed. "Guys, this is our year! I feel it in my bones!"

"Plus, our buddy over here has everything we can only wish we had," Lamont said stepping into the conversation. "He was made the star player of the football team, and he has Stella Eaves." He turned to his friend. "How are things with Stella, by the way?"

"Things are going really great with her," he smirked.

"I still don't know how you did it," William said.

"What do you mean by that?" Brian asked.

"Nothing bad. It's just, well, Stella is beautiful, and she probably has so many guys going after her, especially with those brown eyes, deep brown skin, and black hair. I mean, she's gorgeous. She's been known to turn them all down. How were you the one who managed to get her to say yes?"

Brian shrugged. "Who can really say no to the star football player in this school? Guess even Stella couldn't resist the fact when I asked her out."

"He's got a point," Lamont said. "He even beat Victor to get his position. Any girl would be stupid to turn down being his girlfriend. Right?"

Brian was about to answer when there was a commotion down the hall that caught his attention. "What the..." He turned.

"What's going on?" Eric asked.

"The bus just got here. Remember when we had to take the bus because we weren't old enough to drive?" Brian laughed.

"Let's go see them and have some fun," William suggested.

Brian led his group of friends towards the front door where the younger students and those who didn't have cars were walking in. He rubbed his hands, the smile never leaving his face. "Look at that freak." He pointed to one of the younger students getting off the bus.

"Why is he even allowed in our school?" William asked. "He doesn't look like he's a special needs student."

"Whatever his reason is for being on the special needs bus, let's give him the official welcome back to Ocean Bay High," Brian suggested. "Hey! Kid!" The student slowly turned around, a scared look on his face as he stared at Brian and didn't say a word. "I said hey!" Brian said again. "Don't you know it's impolite to ignore a senior? Not going to say anything? I'm not going to hurt you." Brian laughed. "All I wanted to do was welcome you back to school." He opened his arms wide. "Welcome back, FREAK!"

The students surrounding Brian and his friends turned to the young student, pointing and laughing at him, chanting "freak." Brian turned to his group and smiled. "I don't know about you, but I think I gave this kid a pleasant welcome. He should be good and ready for the new year. Don't you agree?"

"Are you really going to let him go?" William asked.

"How long have you known me, William? I've only just begun." Brian got closer to the student. "We have to let someone like him know that he has no place in our school."

Sam Granillo was a sophomore at Ocean Bay and dealt with this kind of bullying from Brian last year. All summer, he wished Brian would change and never bother him again, but now he knew he was wrong. He turned away from Brian's glare and looked outside where he saw the other students getting off the bus, wishing they were allowed to be on the regular bus with the students and not their own, bringing more attention to themselves. *One. Two. Three. Four.* Sam started counting the students leaving the special needs bus, ignoring Brian.

"Kid! Hey, freak!" Brian yelled in Sam's ear. "Did you

forget the rules over the summer? When I speak to you, you look at me!" Brian turned to his friends, shaking his head. "You'd think he learned his lesson after last year."

"Maybe he needs a reminder of who we are," Lamont said, rubbing his hands together.

Brian put his hand out, stopping his friend before he went after Sam. "Now, it's only the first day of school. There's no need for violence." Brian turned to Sam. "Not right now, at least. You see, our little buddy over here only needs to remember when a senior asks him a question, he needs to answer." He turned to see what caught Sam's attention. "Wish you were outside with your little friends and not stuck here with me?"

Sam continued to ignore Brian and opened up his backpack, taking out an electronic device. He typed on it and soon, in an electronic voice, the device said, "Class time."

"Does he really think I'm still going to fall for this act? Using this thing because he doesn't want to talk to me?"

"If you ask me, I don't think he's learned his lesson from last year," William said.

"Wait! I know what he's trying to tell me," Brian told his friends. "He's telling us we need to leave the halls and get to class because the bell's going to ring soon." He turned to Sam. "Let's get one thing straight. You don't tell me when I'm supposed to go to class. I'm a senior. We're all seniors." He gestured to his friends. "Does any of this make sense to you?"

Sam continued to ignore Brian and kept pointing at his

device. Brian shook his head, annoyed by Sam, and he turned to his friends. "Can you believe this kid?"

"If you ask me, they never should've accepted him here," Eric said. "Hey, why are you even over here with us? Shouldn't you be with your little friends over there?" he said to Sam, pointing to the other students getting off the bus.

Sam looked out the window, a frown on his face. He knew those students from riding on the bus with them every day, but he wouldn't say he was friends with them. The couple of friends he had were students from his math class.

"Hey! Hey!" Brian was shouting. Sam turned around and stared at him, blinking his eyes. "Guess I'm going to get nowhere with you. Fine. Whatever." He bent down to Sam's level. "Just get away from me, freak. Oh, and before you go, I want you to remember one thing."

Sam looked up at Brian. Brian saw the look of fear on Sam's face and laughed.

"For the next year, my friends and I rule the school. Stay clear of us and there won't be any trouble. Got that?"

Brian's friends laughed at Sam when they saw his lips pout and he began to whimper. "I think you finally got to him." William laughed.

Brian sighed, having enough of Sam. There were others in the school he could use to ensure his status in this school, and he wasn't going to waste his first day of his senior year on Sam. "You were so excited to get to class, why are you still standing here? Go on, scat," he threatened Sam.

Sam reached into his backpack, took out his algebra

textbook, and ran off before Brian and his friends could say anything else. He could hear Brian and his friends laughing at him down the hall as he rushed into the classroom. He took a seat in the back of the classroom, hoping he could forget about the greeting he got this morning.

Brian watched as Sam went into his classroom and turned to his friends. "You know, when I woke up this morning, I knew I was going to have a good day because this is our senior year. What I didn't realize was how good it really was going to be. Who knew we would run into Sam?"

"I really thought he was going to cry," William said.

"I'm surprised he didn't," Brian said.

"What do you say? Think we should head over to class? Or should we look to see who else we can find?" Eric asked.

"We can't waste all morning with the younger students, can we? We have to have something to do at lunch." Brian laughed. "Plus, I want to see if I can find Stella before class starts."

"Good luck. Brian, you have to remember you have a girlfriend who actually likes school and study. She's not like any of the other girls you dated," Lamont reminded him. "She's probably in class already."

"Lamont's right. How did you manage to get Stella to be your girlfriend? She never struck me as the kind who would date a jock," William said.

Brian shrugged. "I'm just as shocked as you are that she actually said yes when I asked her to be my girlfriend. But you know, she was made head cheerleader this year. What kind of star football player would I be if I wasn't dating a cheerleader? I've never dated a studious girl before. It's different for me, but I always love a challenge." He saw the principal walking down the hall. "I think we better get to class before he sees us standing here. We already know he hates me."

The four boys said their goodbyes and made plans to meet up at lunch to discuss the upcoming game this weekend. But Brian had Stella on his mind, and he couldn't wait to see her this afternoon.

Chapter Two

When Stella thought about her senior year, she never imagined it was going to be like this. She was head cheerleader; a position she didn't think she would get. Not when there were others who were better than she was at cheering. And here she was, not only head cheerleader but also the girlfriend of Brian Vance. They'd started dating after the last day of school and Brian asked her to be his girlfriend at the beginning of the summer. The two of them spent most of the summer together, when Brian wasn't busy playing football with his friends, and she wasn't with her group of friends from cheerleading. On top of everything else, she tried out for this year's school musical and was waiting for the results to be posted. She walked into the cafeteria and looked to see where her friends were sitting.

Taking a deep breath, her eyes scanned the room until she saw her friends sitting at a table. They were all talking, none noticing she walked in. *They're busy talking about the game this weekend,* she told herself and grabbed a tray off the counter. She looked down at the chickpea salad the lunch lady put on her tray. *At least they decided to start giving us healthy lunches.* She could hear the other students complaining, wanting the unhealthy food options back, but she didn't mind. As a cheerleader, she welcomed the new food.

Eyes were all on her as she started to make her way towards the table where her friends Chelsea, Jodie, Katie, Tallulah, and Alison sat. They finally noticed she was there, and they waved her over. Holding her tray with one hand, Stella used her free hand to wave back. Seeing her friends made her feel a little better. Everything else in her life was changing too quickly, but having the same group of friends since freshman year gave her the stability she needed to get through the first day of school.

She knew she probably should have lunch with Brian. Word was all over the school that they were the popular couple, and students expected to always see them together. But lunchtime was always set aside for her and the girls.

"STELLA! STELLA!"

Stella turned in the direction where she heard her name being called. She sighed when she saw Brian standing up at the table with his friends and waving her over. She gave him a slight wave and continued walking to the other table.

"Stella." Brian rushed to her side. "Where are you going?"

"Over there." She pointed to where her friends sat. Brian yelling her name caused all the students in the cafeteria to look at them in the middle of the room.

"Why?"

"Why? Because it's lunch and the five of us always spend lunch together. We have for the past three years." Stella didn't know why Brian was acting as if this was anything new. They may have only become a couple this summer, but they had known each other since their first day of freshman year.

"Stella." Brian put his arm around Stella's shoulders. "I know you never had a boyfriend before, so this is all new to you. But you're my girlfriend now. And you know what that means? We get to spend lunch together. You'll see your friends at cheerleading practice."

"I always have lunch with them, especially on the first day of school. Besides, they have asked me to eat lunch with them today. Plus, I don't think I'd fit into your table of friends," Stella said.

"Why not?" Brian asked.

"Don't you have the big first game of the year on Friday?"

"Yes, but I don't see what that has to do with anything."

Stella shrugged Brian's arm off her and she turned to look at him. "I know and I'm sorry, but Chelsea said that they needed me to be at lunch today. I don't know why." Stella hoped Brian would be understanding. "Look, she's my best friend. I said that I'd be there. I'm not going to let my best friend down. Next week, I promise I'll sit with you."

"But not today?" Brian asked.

Stella shook her head. "No. I'm sure you and the boys want to discuss playing strategies. And I have to talk to my friends because we have cheerleading tryouts coming up and I'm going to need their help choosing who makes the team. I'll see you after school like we planned."

"Fine." Brian gave up. "After school, then." Sadly, he walked back over to his friends, knowing they saw the whole scene play out.

"What happened over there?" Eric laughed.

Brian shook his head. "Don't ask. Said she wants to go spend lunch with her friends." He rolled his eyes. "We may as well take advantage of this time and discuss our strategy for this weekend's game."

Smiling, Stella walked over to the table where her friends were sitting.

"Stella!" Chelsea, her best friend, jumped up from her seat and ran to her. "What took you so long?"

"Brian stopped me and was hoping to get me to sit with him."

"And why aren't you?" Chelsea asked.

"Because it's the first day of school. What kind of best friend would I be if I decided to go have lunch with my boyfriend instead of with you and the others?" Stella laughed.

"The kind of best friend who knows what's important." Chelsea laughed. "I'm going to guess Brian wasn't too happy with your decision."

"No, but I promised him next week I would have lunch with him. I don't even know why he wanted me at the table with them. They're discussing this weekend's game. What use would I be to them?" Stella shrugged and put her tray down on the table and sat down. "So, are we going to discuss the cheerleading tryouts?"

"That's what you want to talk about?" Jodie asked.

"Well, I assumed that since we have a few spots to fill, we would talk about that." She looked around at her friends. "Why? What else should we talk about?"

"You don't know, do you?" Chelsea smiled.

"Know what?" Stella was confused. "What's going on?"

"Stella, remember last spring when you tried out for the school musical?" Chelsea said.

Stella's heart started to pound. She remembered it all too well. The drama teacher announced last spring that this year's school musical was going to be *Grease*, a movie she absolutely loved and saw over two hundred times. When she heard that announcement, she didn't hesitate to audition as Sandy. There were many times when watching the movie she would act it out, costume and all. "Yes," she answered. She'd been waiting to hear from the drama teacher if she got the part, but she hadn't seen any of the signs posted in the halls. Did her friends know something she didn't?

"Chelsea, you should be the one to give her the news." Katie smiled.

"So, I was walking by the drama room on my way to lunch when I heard Mr. Phelps talking to his assistant. He was giving him the name of the students who made the play and what parts. And guess what I heard?" Chelsea waited a few seconds before continuing the news. "Stella, you're playing Sandy!" She jumped up and squealed.

"I...I..." Stella's jaw dropped. She knew the part of Sandy by heart. She'd impressed Mr. Phelps when she sang "Hopelessly Devoted" for her audition, when the others who tried out to be Sandy sang songs that weren't from *Grease*. This shouldn't have been a surprise, but hearing the words that she got the part was still a shock. "Are you sure?"

"Yes!" Chelsea jumped up and down. "I stayed to make sure I did hear right. He said out of all the girls who auditioned for Sandy, you were the only one he could see playing her on the stage. Have to say, I agree with him. We've gone to the *Grease* sing-along showings together. You're the only one in the theater who belts out the songs." She bent down and hugged Stella. "I'm so happy for you."

"I can't believe this." Stella had tears in her eyes. She'd wanted nothing more than to star in the school musical since her first day in high school. For the past three years, she wasn't sure of her singing or acting and only tried out for parts in the chorus. She didn't expect much when she'd auditioned for Sandy, especially since she never tried out for the lead before, but here she was, starring in the production of Grease. Mr. Phelps must've seen something in her that she never did.

"Well, you better believe it." Chelsea finally sat back down at the table. "We've got a celebrity in our group!"

Stella was hearing the words, but she still couldn't believe the news. Chelsea looked up at Katie and nodded. Katie left the table and returned a few minutes later with a cake in her hands.

"When Chelsea told us the news, I skipped last period to go to the bakery down the block and have this made for you." Katie placed the box down on the table and opened it. Stella smiled seeing the chocolate cake and written in pink frosting was **CONGRATULATIONS, SANDY!** Stella laughed at how they were already calling her Sandy.

"I don't know what to say." Stella was speechless. "And you even had it say 'Sandy' instead of my name."

"Why wouldn't we? You are Sandy, after all." Chelsea laughed. "Let's dig in!"

The girls cut the cake and passed it around to their table, talking about the cheerleading tryouts and the game this weekend. "So, Stella, I have to ask you a question," Katie said. "How does it feel to have this year be your year?"

"My year? I wouldn't say this is my year," Stella said.

"Why not? You're head cheerleader, dating the star football player, and now you can add lead in the school musical to your list. This is totally your year!" Chelsea said.

Stella never thought of it that way. *My year. Maybe they're right. This could be my year.* She smiled at her friends as she continued to eat the cake. "So much for eating healthy." She laughed, pushing away the salad she got for lunch.

"One little slice of cake won't hurt us," Chelsea said. "The game isn't until this weekend anyway. Plus, it is the first day of school, so it's a double celebration. Speaking about this weekend's game, is Brian nervous? All the scouts are going to be there to get him on their radar."

"I really don't know," Stella responded. "If he is, he hasn't said anything to me about being nervous. I don't even think he knows what it feels like to be nervous about anything. Now me, that's a different story."

"What do you mean?" Chelsea asked. "Are you nervous about the play?"

"Oddly enough, that's the only thing in my life I'm not nervous about." Stella laughed. "Cheerleading."

"Why are you nervous about cheerleading? You've been a cheerleader since freshman year. You're going to be great like always." Chelsea tried to cheer up her best friend.

"It was different the past three years because I wasn't the head cheerleader. I am now and that means everything is going to be different. I'll be in the front, rather than behind the other girls like it's always been. Also, I'm going to have to be part of all the decisions when it comes to tryouts and who to let go from the team. And that stress is now going to be added to starring in the school play and being Brian's girlfriend."

"Being Brian's girlfriend is probably going to be the easiest thing this school year," Katie said.

"Are you kidding me?" Stella laughed. "Do you realize now that I'm dating the star football player, people expect to see us together at all times? Why do you think Brian was so upset I came to have lunch with you rather than sit at the table with him and his friends? He said it wouldn't look right for his girlfriend to be sitting with her friends." She rolled her eyes. "Whatever." She shrugged it off. "He has to understand that even though we're a couple, we do have different lives. I would be so out of place at his table. The only thing I know about football is that we cheer at the games. But we do that for basketball and baseball too. It doesn't mean I know everything about the sports." She laughed.

"Still, you have to see it from his point of view. Every

year, the star football player always has a cheerleader on their arm. You rarely see them apart," Katie said.

"Know what I think we should talk about? How she is dating Brian in the first place," Alison suggested and turned to her friend. "I can't believe you're dating him."

"Why is it so hard to believe?" Stella was confused. It wasn't anything new for the power couple in the school to be the current star football player and head cheerleader. This happened every year. When she found out she was promoted to head cheerleader, she knew it was only a matter of time before Brian asked her to be his girlfriend. And she was right. He cornered her in the hall on the last day of school and asked her in front of all his and her friends. Even if she wanted to, she couldn't say no without making a scene.

"I don't mean it in a bad way. It's just shocking, that's all," Alison said. "I mean, you never had a boyfriend before and the first time you get one, it's someone like Brian? In the three years we've been at this school, you've never shown an interest in him. You've never shown an interest in any boy at this school, now that I think about it. I find it odd that you went from never wanting a boyfriend to nabbing the most eligible boy at Ocean Bay High School. Do you know how many girls would die to be in your place right now?"

Stella was getting annoyed by her friend's attitude. She pushed her plate with the slice of cake away from her and stared at Alison. "No, Alison. I don't know. How many?"

"Too many to count, that's for sure," Alison said. "As I said, I'm not trying to be mean. It's just interesting when you think about it. Am I right?" she asked the other girls at the table, who nodded.

"I was surprised," said Tallulah, "because I thought you had better taste than Brian."

"I don't know what you're expecting me to say. You all said it was bound to happen. If that is the case, then it shouldn't be shocking that the two of us are dating now." Looking at Tallulah, she said, "Why am I dating him? Because throughout the summer he was always so thoughtful, caring, and fun. He would always make me feel like I was special and loved. He has a good heart." She got up from her seat and pushed her chair in. "I'll be right back."

"Stella, I'm sorry if I made you upset. You don't have to leave," Alison said.

Stella shook her head. "I have to go call my mom and let her know about getting the lead in the play. And you know they don't allow us to use our cellphones inside the school. I'm just going to step outside for a few." She grabbed her purse and headed out to the schoolyard. Calling her mother could've waited until after school. She pulled her phone out of her bag and called her.

"Stella? Sweetie? How's the first day of school going?" Darlene answered the phone.

"Mom! I got some exciting news! Remember when I auditioned for this year's production of *Grease*?" Stella found it hard to contain her excitement.

"How could I forget? It was all you talked about this summer." Darlene was quiet for a few seconds. "Wait. Weren't you supposed to find out the results today?"

"Yes! I'm playing Sandy. Mom, can you believe it? I'm going to be playing Sandy. I've always dreamed of getting this role since I was a little girl!"

"Sweetie, this is wonderful news. Ever since you first saw the movie, you always pretended to be Sandy whenever we watched it. I don't think they could've found a better Sandy for the production. Know what we'll do? Celebrate this weekend after the game."

"That sounds great, Mom," Stella said.

"How is the rest of the day going?"

"The same as always when it's the first day of school." Stella laughed. "I was at lunch when I found out the news about the play and I couldn't wait to tell you the news."

"I won't keep you. I'm sure you want to finish lunch before your next class. I'll call your father and let him know the great news."

"Can I tell him myself tonight? I want to see his reaction." Stella looked at the clock and realized she better get back or she'd end up being late for study hall. "I'll see you at home later." She said goodbye, putting her phone back in her bag and walking back into the cafeteria.

Stella headed back to the table where she'd sat earlier with her friends and saw only her food was left on the table. The girls left without telling her, and she didn't know where they went, except Jodie who she noticed was at the vending machine. She quickly grabbed her phone, hoping she wouldn't get caught, and checked to see if she'd missed a text from Chelsea that they left. She threw her phone back in her bag when she didn't see any messages. She looked down at her half-eaten salad and cake and picked it up, suddenly losing her appetite. *So much for us always sticking together. She* laughed to herself wondering why she believed that pact in the first place.

I guess it wouldn't hurt for me to go sit with Brian now. She was making her way to his table when she saw Brian and his friends get up from the table. *Or not.* She sighed. The boys didn't have a care in the world as they laughed and punched each other on the arms. *And he thought I wanted to sit with them?* She knew the other guys had girlfriends and none of them were sitting at the table. What made Brian think she would've been comfortable being the only girl at the table?

Brian looked up and his eyes caught Stella standing alone. She gave him a small smile, and he gave her a quick wave before going back to his friends.

Stella watched as a student she'd never noticed before walked towards Brian and his friends. She didn't know why she stayed put, but something told her not to move. There was something in Brian's eyes as he saw the boy walking towards them that Stella felt she needed to see.

"Hey, look who made another appearance!" Brian said loud enough for everyone in the cafeteria to hear. "It's our buddy, Sam!" he said to his friends. "Who knew we would be lucky enough to see him twice in one day?"

Sam tried to walk quickly, covering his face with his hands to protect himself from the football players. Stella studied him, noticing his dark hazel eyes that had sadness in them. *What is Brian doing to this poor boy?* Based on what Brian announced and the way the boy looked terrified, she thought they must've had a run-in earlier today.

Jodie, put her hand on Stella's shoulder. "Guess Brian found the one he's going to pick on this year."

"What do you mean?" Stella asked.

"Watch. You'll see what I mean."

"What are you doing here, freak?" Brian poked Sam on the chest. "Didn't I tell you to stay away from us?"

Sam took his AAC device out of his bag. "Not this again." Brian laughed. "We're going to be here forever."

The device said, "Lunchtime." Brian swiped the device, taking it out of Sam's hand and holding it over his head. Sam started madly jumping for it and hitting out at Brian.

"Careful now, Sam. You will get into trouble if you hit me. Now remember your place. He dropped the device on the ground but pushed Sam away from it. Sam was now shaking and sat huddled, covering himself with his hands.

"Lunchtime. I don't care. Just stay out of our faces."

"This is what I was talking about," Jodie said. "Brian always finds some poor kid from the special needs group to pick on. And then he does whatever he can to make their lives miserable for the year. Though, now that I think about it, I think this is the same one he picked on last year. Oh, well." Jodie shrugged. "I'm going to head out. See you after school."

Stella couldn't believe what she was seeing and felt sick to her stomach. She'd never seen this side of Brian before. She watched as the poor boy tried to get away from Brian, but he wasn't letting him get away that easily. And she wasn't going to stand to see this happen for another second.

She walked over to Brian and tapped him hard on the shoulder. "Why don't you leave him alone?"

Brian briefly stopped taunting Sam when he recognized the voice coming from behind him. He turned around with a scowl on his face. "What do you think you're doing?" he said to Stella.

"Getting you to stop picking on this boy. What did he ever do to you?" Stella crossed her arms.

"What I'm doing to him is none of your business. You have no right to come over to me and talk to me this way." Brian was shocked by his girlfriend's behavior. No girlfriend of his had the right to tell him he couldn't pick on students like Sam.

"It is my business when I see you threatening someone. All he was doing was trying to walk past the group of you and you went after him. And why? Because he's not part of your group? I never knew you could be like this."

"Well, you better get used to it because this is who I am," Brian said.

"If this is who you really are, then we aren't going to work out." Stella shook her head.

"What do you mean?"

"Brian, if you're the type of person who picks on someone just because they're different, then it's over between us. I won't date someone who is a bully."

Brian turned to his friends. "Can you believe this? She's actually telling me how to act." He turned back to Stella. "How about you stop causing such a scene? You should've known this is the kind of person I am when you agreed to be my girlfriend."

"If I knew you were a bully, I never would have agreed to be your girlfriend." She got between Sam and Brian so her boyfriend would stop picking on him. "How about you just let him go and not bother him again?" she said to Brian.

"Boo-hoo." Brian pretended to cry. "You've been here since freshman year. You can't tell me you didn't know what kind of guy I was." He rolled his eyes.

Stella was hoping Jodie was wrong. "Why do you have to bully those who are special needs?" Her voice was calm, wanting to get a straight answer out of Brian.

"They shouldn't be here, that's why."

"Why not?" Stella snapped. "They have every right to be here just as much as we do. They're no different than we are."

"No different?" Brian laughed. "Now that's funny. If they weren't different from us, then why do they have to come to school on a different bus? Do we carry around a weird device that talks for us?"

"Look." Stella took a deep breath and let out a loud sigh. "I don't want to fight."

"Listen to me." Brian bent down to Stella's height. "You don't tell me what to do. I think I'm starting to see why your friends decided to leave you when you went outside. I'm tired of picking on Sam for one day," he smirked. He glared at Stella. "And hopefully you'll remember not to tell me what to do again." He turned to his friends. "Let's go," he said.

She didn't need to look to know everyone was staring at her after what they witnessed. No one ever spoke to Brian the way she did. Shaking her head, she saw the poor boy was now huddled on the floor, terrified. She walked over to him and squatting down, gave him a soft smile.

"Sam, was it?" Her voice was gentle. The boy looked up at Stella and slowly nodded. Stella picked up the device that Brian had dropped on the floor. She handed it to him, and she noticed how much his hands shook as he took it. Stella's heart broke when she saw how scared Sam was after Brian's threats. "Let me apologize for his behavior. He had no right to treat you that way. Are you alright?"

Sam slowly nodded his head and stepped away from the wall. He looked around, checking to make sure Brian and his friends weren't in the cafeteria. Stella gently placed a hand on his shoulder. "Don't worry. They're gone. And they won't bother you again. I'll make sure of it."

"Why don't we leave?" she told Sam. He had tears in his eyes, and she wanted to get him out of the cafeteria before other students started teasing him.

The two of them stepped out into the hall. Sam dried his eyes and opened up his device. "Again, I am sorry for what Brian did to you. Did I hear him right? Did he bully you earlier, too?"

Briefly, Sam looked up from his backpack and nodded. He went back to the device. He put up a finger, indicating he wanted Stella to stay for a few minutes. "Thank You," came from the device.

"You're very welcome," Stella said. She didn't know why he didn't talk or why he was using a device. He had something that made him non-verbal, and it broke her heart even more knowing what must've been going through his mind while Brian and his friends were tormenting him.

"Sam, what class do you have next?" she asked. He responded by showing her his schedule. She looked at it and smiled. "English with Mr. Aguilar. I had him last year. You'll do great in his class. Are you alright to go to class?"

Sam didn't answer and Stella wondered if he was worried about running into Brian in the halls. She didn't blame him. She'd heard the threats; it was no wonder Sam would be afraid of being alone walking to class. And from the way things looked, Stella didn't think Sam had any friends. "Tell you what, I'll walk you to your class. That way you won't have to worry about Brian."

Stella walked him to the class, and she didn't leave until she saw him go inside the classroom and take his seat. He gave her a smile and a wave, and she started to head towards the library where she had study hall, but she realized that she had to go speak to the principal, Mr. Richmond, and report Brian's behavior.

She walked into the office where she was greeted by the secretary Mrs. Graves, who had been at the school for decades.

"Stella, what a pleasure to see you." She smiled. Stella was known in the office for all her volunteer work. "What can I do for you today?"

"Is Mr. Richmond free? I need to speak to him about something important."

"Let me go check. What is this about? Is something wrong with your schedule?" Mrs. Graves asked.

"Nothing like that. I wish it was as simple as a mistake in a schedule. But I would like to report bullying I saw during lunch." Stella couldn't believe she was standing here about to report her boyfriend to the principal. What other choice did she have?

"Bullying?" Mrs. Graves shook her head. "There's far too much of that going on here in the school. Wait right here and I'll let Mr. Richmond know you're here."

Stella stood in the office lobby waiting for Mrs. Grave to come back, thinking of how she was going to explain everything to Mr. Richmond. She had a feeling Brian wasn't going to get in much trouble. Not when he was the star football player, and he was needed for this weekend's game. The least she could do is make the principal aware of what was going on. She clenched her hands together, noticing that she was shaking.

Mrs. Graves walked back into the lobby and gestured for her to go into Mr. Richmond's office. "Thank you for bringing it to our attention." Mrs. Graves gave her a small smile and returned to her desk.

"Stella, have a seat," Mr. Richmond welcomed her into his office. "Mrs. Graves tells me you want to report an incident of bullying you witnessed."

"Yes," her voice shook as she took a seat. "During lunch, I saw Brian bullying this student from the special needs group. Sam is his name. And from what I saw, I think Brian was bothering him earlier today."

"I could imagine how hard it was for you to come and report this, especially since Brian is your boyfriend. I will speak to him about his behavior and give him a detention for next week. Unfortunately, that is all I can do at the moment. There would be an uproar if I took him out of this weekend's game or kicked him off the team. I also will make a note and make sure it doesn't get out of hand."

Stella got up from the seat and nodded. The results were

just as she'd expected and there wasn't anything else she could do. "Thank you, Mr. Richmond. I know your hands are tied in a situation like this, but I just wanted to bring it to your attention. I did make sure the student was fine after the altercation and walked him to his class."

"I appreciate it. Let me assure you that we take bullying seriously, regardless if it is by one of the football team," Mr. Richmond said. She left the office, feeling sorry for Sam and all the other students like him who Brian thought he had the right to bully.

Chapter Three

Stella couldn't get the incident in the cafeteria off her mind as she managed to make it through the rest of the first day of school. She was mad at Brian and at his friends for thinking there was nothing wrong with how Brian and the other team members bullied the students. Most of all, she was angry with herself for not finding out what kind of guy Brian really was before she became his girlfriend. That's what disgusted her, how she was going to go through her senior year as the girlfriend of the school bully.

She was walking back to her locker to grab her books when she passed by a student she'd never seen before. He looked at her and smiled. "Excuse me, you don't know me, but I'm new to the school," the boy said. "My name is Jake."

"Stella." She smiled and shook his hand, unsure why he was stopping her out of nowhere.

"You probably think I'm some weirdo stopping you in the middle of the hallway when you want to get home. I just wanted to say, I saw what you did in the cafeteria today."

"Let me guess, you're going to say I was wrong for telling Brian off?" Stella was expecting this from the students. She'd already heard them whispering behind her back when she had classes during the second half of the day.

"What?" Jake was surprised by what she said. "No, that's not at all why I stopped you. I wanted to tell you that I think what you did was very brave."

"Really? You thought I was brave?" Stella didn't go up to Brian to stop the bullying to gain attention. She did it because it was the right thing to do.

"I've been to many different schools, and I've never seen anyone stick up for a student they didn't know. And on top of it, this guy is the star football player. But you didn't care. You defended that boy."

"It was nothing. I can't stand bullying, and I had to put an end to it, or at least try to." She shrugged. She was still upset that Brian was going to get away with what happened today because the principal didn't want to make Brian lose his position on the football team. "Sadly, I don't think Brian is going to stop bullying Sam or any student who's different."

"But you tried, and that's more than I've seen anyone do." Jake smiled. "It was a really great thing you did."

"Thank you." Stella smiled. "And welcome to our school." She continued walking to her locker.

Jake watched Stella as she walked away.

"So, who was that you were talking to?" Henry, Jake's

friend, walked up next to him. It was funny how things changed for Jake since this morning. When he arrived here, he was new and had no friends. Henry was the first student to introduce himself to Jake and show him how to get to his classes and they instantly became friends.

"That's the girl from the cafeteria I told you about," Jake said.

"Oh, that girl!" Henry smiled. "The one you kept talking about during class?"

"Henry, you had to see what she did. She went up to that football player and told him off for bullying that kid."

"Do you have any idea who that was you were just talking to?" Henry asked.

"She said her name is Stella."

"Jake, that was Stella Eaves. She's the head cheerleader. And that football player you saw her confronting is her boyfriend, Brian Vance. Do you realize you went up to one of the most popular girls in the school without being nervous?"

"You're kidding, right?" Jake couldn't believe what he was hearing. Here he was, a new student in this school and he'd managed to make a friend on his first day and talk to the head cheerleader.

"You've got guts. I've never spoken to her. I mean, I'm sure you can tell I'm not exactly the most popular guy here." Henry laughed.

"Neither am I." Jake chuckled. "Henry, I need to head home." He excused himself grabbing his backpack from his locker. He said goodbye to his friend and headed to his car.

Jake's mind was preoccupied as he drove home,

thinking about Stella. He sighed with relief when he saw no one was home, giving him time to be alone. *She is the head cheerleader. And she stuck up for a student she didn't know. Amazing.* Jake still found it hard to believe what happened today. The way Stella spoke to Brian, Jake never would've guessed she was his girlfriend. But what caught his attention was how she was willing to get in the middle of the bullying and put an end to it.

It was odd for him to be alone at home, but today was one of the days his brother was at school later than usual and his parents were at work. He was going to use the opportunity to his advantage and get his homework started before his family came home. Today was the first day of school and it meant nothing to these teachers, as he learned quickly when he received homework during his first class.

Jake found it hard to concentrate on his work. The events of the day kept playing in his mind. *That poor boy.* He shook his head thinking back to how scared Sam looked in the cafeteria. Jake hated bullying, and he wished he'd thought to stick up for Sam, the way Stella did. And now, he regretted not being by her side, so she wasn't fighting this battle on her own.

He jumped up when he heard the front door open and his brother Jasper ran into the house, giving Jake a tight hug. "You're home!" Jasper was excited.

"You knew I had to be home before you so I could hear all about your first day of school." Jake smiled. He looked up as his mother walked inside.

"Jake, you're home." Ashley smiled at her son. "How

was your first day? I know it must've been tough starting a new school in your senior year."

"Mom, I can honestly tell you it went better than I ever expected. Oh, and I already made a friend. He said he'll introduce me to his friends at the game this weekend." Jake left out the events of the day, but he had a feeling this was going to be the first time he didn't mind transferring to a new school.

When Friday rolled around, everyone was settled into the new school year more or less. To the football players, the only important thing on their minds was the big game tonight. They didn't care about homework, nor did the teachers bother them if it wasn't done. The first game of the year was always big news and everyone in town was at the football field on Friday night.

I shouldn't be here, Stella thought as she took her place in the front line of cheerleaders. The game was almost over with their school in the lead. They were cheering the players, but Stella's heart wasn't in it. Not anymore. The last two years, she'd loved being a cheerleader, but this year, something was different, and it was within her. *I don't fit in with these girls.* It was a hard fact she had to face, but she'd realized earlier this week in the cafeteria when they left her alone, she was a different person.

The field erupted in screams as Brian scored the final touchdown. Their team had won, and Stella had to lead the squad with the victory cheer. Everyone started to gather on the field to congratulate the players, while Stella was pushing her way through the crowd to get out of there.

"Hey! Where are you going?" Chelsea ran up to Stella. "We're all going to go out to celebrate the win!"

"I think I'm going to skip out on this celebration," Stella said. She wanted to go find her family and leave.

"Stella, are you crazy? Your boyfriend scored the winning touchdown! Everyone is going to expect you to be with him when we celebrate."

"Technically, he didn't score the winning touchdown since we were winning from the beginning," Stella said. "There has been a lot on my mind this week and I just want to get home. Tell everyone I'll see them on Monday." Stella left before Chelsea could try and get her to stay. "Mom. Dad. There you are." She saw them with her twin brothers, Abraham and Joseph, standing at the entrance of the field.

"Stella, we assumed you were going to stay and celebrate with everyone," Darlene said.

"Mom, don't you remember you said we could celebrate my getting the lead in the play tonight? I'd rather go home and celebrate with all of you instead of going out with them." She pointed to the students on the field.

Darlene and James gave each other looks, surprised their daughter didn't want to be with her friends. "Stella, are you sure?" Darlene asked. "When I suggested we celebrate after the game, I forgot you may want to go out with your friends."

"Mom, really, I want to go home and celebrate." That was no lie. After discovering what kind of person Brian was, Stella didn't want to spend much time with him or her friends. They didn't understand why she was upset with Brian's behavior. She didn't want to be around people who were blind to the problem of bullying, and she was upset with them for their attitude.

"As long as you're sure, then let's go," James said. "We did have a cake made for you in honor of being Sandy."

Stella was happy when her parents didn't press the issue. The five of them returned home where they celebrated her getting the lead in the play. Sitting on the couch, eating her cake, Stella watched her brothers, Abraham and Joseph, talking and goofing off. She tried to think back to when she was their age, not even a teenager yet, and life seemed simple. Her brothers didn't have to worry about the problems of high school for another few years.

She loved how close her family was, and she could talk to them about anything that was on her mind. She wanted to tell them about the first day of school and what she'd discovered about Brian, but tonight wasn't the night to bring up that topic. She hoped they could help her out with what she should do next. Did she really want to continue dating Brian? No. She didn't hesitate to come up with that answer. How to end things with him? That was a different matter.

Chapter Four

Stella woke up Saturday morning, feeling better than she had all week. After celebrating with her parents the night before, she'd lay in her bed, looking up at the ceiling unable to stop thinking about Brian, cheerleading, the school year as a whole. She knew she no longer wanted to be Brian's girlfriend. She didn't want to be associated with someone like him. And once the news came out she didn't want to be with him, she knew some of her so-called friends would turn on her, but she didn't care. All she had to figure out was when and how she was going to call it off with Brian once and for all.

After a night of tossing and turning, she pulled herself out of bed and got herself ready for the day. She took a look in the mirror, and smiled, happy with the decisions she was making with her life.

She walked downstairs to find her parents getting breakfast on the table. "Morning, Mom. Morning, Dad!" Stella hugged them. "Where are Abraham and Joseph?"

"Still asleep. Think they had a little too much cake last night and the sugar high got the best of them." Darlene laughed. "Let them sleep it off. Plus, they're probably still tired from the first week of school."

Stella grabbed a plate and sat at the kitchen table. Darlene and James looked at each other, expecting their daughter to be more excited. The girl sitting at the table didn't look like one who'd landed the lead role in the school play. "Stella, is everything alright?" James asked.

"Everything is great, Dad. Why do you ask?"

"Your mother and I were talking last night, and we find it odd that you aren't as excited as we thought you would be about getting the role of Sandy. We thought you would be happy considering how much you love *Grease*."

"I am happy. Believe me, I am." Stella was afraid of this happening. Her parents always knew when something was weighing heavily on her mind.

"Then what's wrong? You haven't mentioned it since you called me with the news," Darlene said.

"Mom, it's nothing to do with the play. I've had a lot on my mind. Some things I needed to work on. But I think I've gotten it all figured out. I hope."

"Stella." Darlene sat next to her. "We can't help but think there's something wrong."

"Your mother is right." James sat on the other side of Stella. "We're not only talking about your lack of excitement for the play but also what happened last night. Why were you in such a rush to come home? You know we would've allowed you to go out with your friends."

"I know, but..." Stella paused. Did she really want to tell

her parents what was going on? "I've been rethinking a lot of choices I made since this summer." She looked down at her plate of food.

"Such as?" Darlene asked.

"First, I'm wondering if cheerleading really is for me." Saying those words brought great satisfaction to Stella. She did cheerleading in elementary school, and it was a given she would continue once she reached high school. But was cheerleading all there was to life? At one point she thought this was what she wanted. Now, she was beginning to realize there was more she wanted to do, and cheerleading was going to hold her back.

"You know we would never force you to do anything you didn't want to," Darlene said. "But I thought you loved being a cheerleader?"

"So did I." Stella chuckled. "In this week alone, I realized the cheerleaders' attitudes aren't the same as mine. I don't think I fit in with them the way I once did."

"Have you talked to Brian about this?" James asked. "Something tells me he isn't going to like it when you tell him you don't want to be a cheerleader."

"Him?" Stella laughed. "He's another story and also part of the reason why I don't want to be a cheerleader anymore."

"The two of you couldn't stay away from each other this summer. What happened?" Darlene asked. "I thought you were happy with him."

"Let's just say the Brian I knew this summer isn't the real Brian. Look, I know I won't be able to just up and quit cheerleading. I'll stay until they find another girl to take my place, but I don't want to be near Brian more than I have to be."

James and Darlene looked at each other. "Care to elaborate?" Darlene asked.

Stella shook her head. "Let's just say Brian did something I never thought he would. The girls told me it shouldn't bother me, and I shouldn't have been surprised. But I am. Not once during this summer did he show this side of him. I'm beginning to wonder if I was so blind these past three years. How could I not see it before?"

"When you said he did something—" Darlene began when James jumped into the conversation.

"Did that boy hurt you?" Anger rose in James' face. "I swear if he hurt you I'm going to—"

"Dad, no," Stella stopped him. "That isn't what I meant. I would never let him hurt me. But he did hurt someone else, and it really bothered me," Stella admitted. Every time she'd seen Sam in the hall this week her heart went out to him, knowing he was still on Brian's list of students to taunt.

James started to calm down hearing that his daughter wasn't hurt by her boyfriend, but it didn't make him feel completely better seeing how upset Stella was at Brian. He took a deep breath and slowly exhaled before he continued. "I'm glad he didn't hurt you. I would've been at his door in a second if he did. But clearly whoever he bothered upsets you."

"It did." Stella felt tears in her eyes as she replayed the incident in her head. The terrified look on Sam's face was still there when she saw him days later. "Dad, Brian is a bully. It was horrible what I saw him do. And what's worse is since he's the star football player the principal won't do much about it."

"Sweetie, you know you can tell us anything," Darlene said. "Maybe you'll feel a little better if you tell us what it was you saw Brian do."

Stella thought about it. If there was anyone who would listen to what she had to say, it was her parents. She hadn't told anyone but that new student, Jake, why she stood up to Brian and keeping it inside was eating her up. She closed her eyes for a few seconds, gathering her thoughts.

"There was this boy, younger than us. I think he's a sophomore." She shook her head, getting off-topic. "That's not important. What you need to know is this boy is in the special needs classes in our school and he has autism. Brian thought because he's different from the rest of us, it gives him the right to bully the kid. Jodie told me Brian bullied this kid last year too. Again, I can't believe I never saw it until now. But it was horrible. The poor kid wanted to get away and go have his lunch, but Brian and his friends wouldn't allow it. I waited to see if anyone was going to put a stop to it, but when no one did, I went up and confronted Brian." She started crying as she continued to tell her parents what happened. "The insults they spewed at him were disgusting."

Stella's parents put their arms around their daughter as she cried. "You stood up to Brian?" James was in shock.

"He wasn't happy when I told him to stop bullying Sam, that's for sure." She gave a nervous laugh. "Word got around what I did, and the other cheerleaders were mad at me for doing that. They said I should've left it alone because I'm his girlfriend. But how could I? The young girls in the school see me as a role model being the head cheerleader. I couldn't let Brian get away with bullying. I went to see the principal after, but he gave me the usual excuse that they would make note of it. I knew what he really meant. He wasn't going to do anything because the school needs Brian on the team. And this is why I don't think I want to be a cheerleader anymore and I most definitely don't want to be Brian's girlfriend."

"Stella, I don't know what to say other than your mother and I are very proud of you," James said. "You saw a student who needed help, and you went up there to defend him without caring about yourself first or what others would say."

"Your father is right. Why didn't you tell us about this on Monday when it happened?" Darlene asked.

"Honestly, I don't know. I think I wanted to take time to think everything over. When the girls started telling me how wrong it was for me to confront Brian, I started to believe them. But now I see how they were the ones who were wrong. They think that because he's the star football player, he's beyond reproach."

"Now, I see why you want no part of any of them," Darlene said. "And we support your decision."

"Thank you." Stella smiled. "Can I ask you both a question? What exactly is autism? I know this kid has it, but I never met anyone who acts in the way he does before. He wouldn't even speak to me. He only communicated with a device."

"Sweetie, there are different forms of autism," James said. "It's not easy to answer a question like that."

"From what you just said, it sounds like this student is non-verbal," Darlene added.

Stella nodded. Everything was becoming clearer about why Sam didn't say a word when she was talking to him. "That makes sense. When he wanted to thank me for sticking up for him, he used a device to talk for him. I asked what class he had next, and he showed me his schedule. I didn't realize there were so many different forms of autism."

"It's called a spectrum. Everyone with autism is affected differently. And every day there is more research being done about it," Darlene said. "The device he used is called an AAC device."

"I have an idea," James said. "I feel like you may want to help others that are like Sam. Why don't you go research the topic?"

"That's a great idea." Stella jumped out of her seat. "I think I'll walk to the library and get some books on it. Unless you need me to stay home today to watch the boys?"

"You go. Maybe you'll find some organizations you can volunteer for that will help you learn more about autism," Darlene suggested.

"That's a great idea! Once I quit cheerleading, I'll have more free time for the play and for volunteer work. Thank you, Mom and Dad." She hugged her parents.

"Do you want to take the car?" James asked.

"Not today. I think I'm going to walk to the library. And

maybe after I spend some time there, I'll take a walk on the beach. That always helps to clear my mind."

Stella said goodbye to her parents and headed to the library, ready to spend the morning there to get as much research done as she could. She really liked the suggestion from her parents about doing volunteer work to help autistic kids. Everything was finally starting to fall into place.

S tella's parents were right, there was so much information on autism she never knew existed. After spending the morning in the library, she walked back home to drop off the books she'd checked out. When she arrived at the library, she had no idea she was going to be looking through so many books and she didn't want to carry them with her on the beach.

"That's a lot of books." James helped his daughter bring the books into the house.

"Once I started reading up on autism, I couldn't stop. Oh, and I didn't tell you the best part. The library is connected to autism programs throughout the neighborhood. I signed up for their volunteer list and the librarian said I'll be getting a call when one of the places is looking for volunteers."

"Stella, I know I said this to you earlier, but I'm going to say it again. Your mother and I are so proud of you." He hugged his daughter. "Are you off to the beach now?"

"Yes. I still need time to think everything over when it

comes to cheerleading and Brian, though I'm sure my decision has been made. But you know how the beach always clears my mind."

"Go and enjoy your time. You had a pretty hectic week, you deserve to have time to yourself," James said.

Stella gave her father another hug before leaving the house and heading to the beach. The beach was empty, surprising Stella. It was early on a Saturday afternoon and usually crowded on a fall day like today, but she welcomed the quiet. All she could hear was the sound of the waves crashing on the shore.

Making her way down to the ocean, Stella took her shoes off and let the waves wash over her feet. Ever since she was a child and her parents brought her to the beach for the first time, years before her brothers were born, she always found this scenery relaxing.

She looked at the waves and started to think about the past week. *What is wrong with me?* She started to question every decision she'd made since the last day of school the year before. That day in June, she thought she knew what she wanted for the rest of her high school career. Three months later and the only thing she was certain about was that she wanted to be in the school musical. But when it came down to Brian and cheerleading, those were part of her past.

There were so many things she was going to have to take care of when she went back to school on Monday. She would have to go see the moderator of the cheerleaders and let her know her decision. Hopefully, she would be able to find a replacement soon so Stella could leave the squad and concentrate only on the play.

And then, there was Brian. She definitely didn't want to stay his girlfriend now that she knew what kind of guy he was and how he treated people who were different. She knew she shouldn't blame herself for never seeing it before, but she did. *How did I not know he was a bully? The other girls knew, but I didn't.* Was she so infatuated with him that she was blind to it all?

Well, I can't think of that anymore, Stella said to herself, getting up and wiping the sand off her dress. She was glad she'd decided to come to the beach. It was exactly what she needed. Monday morning, she would take care of business, including breaking up with Brian.

I really am a new person, she thought heading back home. She knew people changed as they got older, but she didn't expect to go through it until she was in college. There was a time when she would've been afraid of such a change, but now she welcomed it. Thinking back to last year, she realized she was much happier when she was single. *No wonder I didn't have an interest in dating any of the boys from our school. Being in a relationship is too stressful.* She laughed to herself. Monday morning, she would prepare herself to lose the friends she'd made in cheerleading once they found out her decisions.

Chapter Five

The weekend went too quickly for Stella's liking. Even though she had her mind set on what she was going to do, it didn't make it any easier. She decided not to wait until Monday to call it off with Brian and met up with him on Sunday to deliver the news. As expected, he wasn't too pleased and begged for her to think it over. But Stella's decision was final. She could never date someone who was a bully. Once Brian realized Stella wasn't going to take him back, he stormed off. Stella thought she would feel upset, even for a short period. Instead, she felt a great sense of relief.

Monday morning, she parked her car in the student parking lot and took a deep breath as she shut off the engine and stepped out of the car. She saw her group of friends waiting on the front lawn, waving her over.

"Hey!" She forced a smile on her face, hoping she didn't give them a reason to think anything was wrong.

"Hey? That's all you've got to say?" Chelsea asked.

"Yeah?" Stella was confused. What else did they expect her to say? She wasn't going to tell them about quitting cheerleading until she spoke to their moderator. "What else would I say?"

"How about you tell us why you left so quickly after the game?" Allison crossed her arms.

Stella was afraid they would bring this up. "I had other things to do."

"Other things to do?" Allison said. "You're the head cheerleader. Do you know what it looked like when we all showed up at the diner and everyone was there but you? Brian wasn't too happy."

Of course, he wasn't. Stella wanted to roll her eyes at Allison's comment. Brian made sure to point that out to her yesterday when they met up. When he blamed her for embarrassing him when she didn't appear at his side during the celebration, he made it easier for her to break up with him.

"What do you want me to say? I had other things to do, and I wanted to go home instead of hanging out. What's wrong with that?"

"Stella," Chelsea's tone was calmer than Allison's. "I know being the center of attention is new and something you don't feel comfortable with, but you have to get used to it. You're Brian's girlfriend now and people expect to see you two together at events, including victory celebrations. You weren't even with him when we all gathered on the field."

Stella debated whether she should tell the girls that she and Brian were no longer a couple, but seeing how they were already trying to make her feel guilty for not attending the celebration, she decided it was better to wait. "If you must know, I went home to celebrate with my family."

"You decided to celebrate the football team winning the big game with your family instead of us?" Allison was confused.

"No. I went to celebrate getting the lead in the school play. I'm sorry I didn't tell you all where I was going when I left. That's the only thing I'll apologize for. But I'm not going to stand here and say I was wrong for going with my family. They wanted to congratulate me on the school play, and I will always choose to spend time with my family over anything else."

"Something isn't right." Allison shook her head. "I feel there's more to this that you aren't telling us. Come on, let's go and get to our lockers before the halls are crowded," she said to the other girls.

"Chelsea, you believe me. Right?" Stella asked. Chelsea was her best friend since they were in the first grade and if there was anyone who would take her side, Stella knew she could count on Chelsea.

"You know I always stick up for you, but Allison is right about this. It's not like you to dismiss your responsibilities. And you knew there were going to be many new ones once you became head cheerleader. Look, I'll talk to Allison, but you're going to have to do your part too. You need to be there for your boyfriend and the rest of us cheerleaders," Chelsea said heading into school.

Stella stood still. She couldn't believe what happened.

Even her best friend wasn't taking her side and she never felt so alone. This morning, she felt bad about wanting to quit cheerleading and suddenly leaving the squad. Now she felt she was totally alone.

Stella went through the day avoiding Brian after yesterday. She was afraid he'd started to spread the word around that they broke up, but when she saw no one was whispering behind her back, she knew their breakup was still a secret. Well, until she told the girls, which was going to happen soon as they met up for lunch. Whatever was bothering the other cheerleaders this morning disappeared as Chelsea and Katie spoke to her when they passed each other in the halls. The only one who seemed to have a problem with her was Allison, but Stella didn't expect anything else from her. Allison's attitude changed once Stella was chosen over her as head cheerleader. *Soon, you will be able to take my spot, and I won't have to hear you complain about me again.*

She walked into the cafeteria and grabbed her lunch tray avoiding eye contact with Brian's table. She made her way to the table where the cheerleaders sat and took a seat, hoping the events from this morning were all a memory.

"Great! Stella's here! Now we can talk about the party!" Jodie said.

"Party? What party?" Stella asked. She didn't hear about any party during classes.

"What party?" Chelsea playfully slapped her arm. "You

haven't heard about the big party happening this weekend?"

Stella shrugged. "No. Who's having it?"

"Don't remember his name, but it's one of the football players. He said since they won last week's game, they should continue celebrating," Chelsea explained. "If you ask me, I don't care who's throwing it. I'm only interested in partying!"

"Chelsea, why are you bothering trying to convince her to go? We saw this past weekend that Stella doesn't want to hang out with any of us. If she didn't want to go to a simple celebration, why would she come to some unsupervised party a football player is throwing?" Allison glared at Stella and smirked.

"Allison, Stella knows how important it is for her to come to these parties. Right?" Chelsea gave her friend a look.

"What night is the party?" Stella asked. She was prolonging giving them an answer. They weren't going to like it once she told them everything.

"Friday," Allison said.

"Friday?" Stella tapped her fingers on the table. "Yeah, I don't think I'm going to make it."

"WHAT?" Chelsea yelled.

"Ha! I knew it." The smile never left Allison's face when Stella said she was skipping the party. "Know what I think it is? She thinks she's too good to hang out with us."

"That's not true," Stella tried to defend herself. "I never went to parties before. Why would I start now?"

"For one thing, you're Brian's girlfriend," Chelsea said.

"This is what I was talking about this morning with you. You need to be doing things with the rest of us, especially parties Brian is going to be at. Do you realize how bad it'll make you look if you're not there Friday night?"

"I don't think it's going to matter much if I'm there or not," Stella said.

"Are you kidding me? Of course, it will! Everyone remembers how Brian showed up at the celebration alone last Friday. And now you expect him to show up at a party without you? Brian isn't going to take this news very well when he hears you aren't going," Chelsea said.

"Actually, I don't think Brian is going to care if I'm not there either." Stella hoped her choice of words would get her point across to her friends. None of the girls sitting at the table seemed to understand and Stella shook her head. "I broke up with Brian yesterday."

The girls sat silently at the table, trying to take in what Stella announced. Chelsea was the first one to break the silence with a loud laugh. "Stella, that's a good one. You had us almost believing you broke up with Brian. And I know you wouldn't do that without discussing it with us first."

"This isn't a joke," Stella said. "I broke up with him yesterday."

Chelsea and Jodie sat at the table with their jaws dropped from the news. Allison was the only one still sitting there with a smile on her face. "I knew this was going to happen. I just didn't think you would break up with him so soon into the school year. I thought for sure you would've stayed with him until the homecoming dance. You were never the type that would actually want to date an athlete. I don't even know how you made the cheerleading team."

"Wait," Chelsea ignored Allison. "You went and broke up with Brian yesterday? I understand if you didn't want to tell anyone on the cheerleading squad. But I'm your best friend. How could you do something so drastic without telling me first?"

"Because I know you and the others would've said I shouldn't break up with him. This was a decision I had to make on my own. I can't stay with someone like Brian."

"And why not?" Chelsea asked.

"He's not the kind of guy I want to be associated with, that's why!"

"Oh, Stella. You're not still going on about what happened last week in the cafeteria, are you?" Chelsea was disappointed in her best friend. "You know that's how Brian is."

"No! I didn't know that's how Brian was. If I did, I never would've been his girlfriend in the first place. I don't tolerate bullying, and I wasn't going to stay with someone who is a bully. I didn't tell any of you what I was planning because of this reason. None of you saw what was wrong with how Brian treated that poor boy. Oh, and one more thing. As of today, I am no longer going to be a cheerleader. I've realized I don't fit in with any of you."

"Now I know you're losing your mind," Chelsea said. "You love cheerleading!"

"Correction, I loved cheerleading. Or at least I thought I did. And now that I'm the lead in the school play, I want to concentrate on it. And other important things."

"What could be more important than cheerleading?" Chelsea said.

"There are other things in life that are much more important than cheerleading," Stella said.

"You know what?" Allison got up from her seat. "Jodie, Chelsea, let's go find Brian and get some more information on the party. I'm sure he won't mind helping us out now that he's freshly single," she smirked, making sure Stella saw and knew what was going on in her mind.

Stella watched in astonishment as her "friends" made excuses and got up from the table, including Chelsea. "You're going too?" Stella asked.

"Allison's right. We need to go ask Brian something about the party. He may have the information we need."

The girls left, leaving Stella alone with Tallulah at the table. Stella got up and moved closer to her friend. "How come you didn't go with them?"

"Parties aren't my thing," Tallulah said. "And I didn't like how they treated you. I saw what you did last week, sticking up for Sam. I was so glad to see that someone had the guts to do something, no one else did."

"I'm happy someone here feels that way." Stella sighed. "I've heard them talking about me in the halls. Not that I listened to what they said, but it still hurt."

"I don't blame you for quitting cheerleading. I'm not enjoying it too much either," Tallulah admitted. "I have no idea why I tried out in the first place."

"Tallulah, I've been asking myself that same question."

"So, you're in the school musical this year, right?" Tallulah asked.

"I am." Stella smiled. She was glad to have a friend to talk to about how excited she was to have the lead. The other girls were only excited for her on the day she got the news, but a day later, that was pushed aside and the only thing they wanted to talk about was football and cheerleading.

"You must be excited."

"Excited is an understatement." Stella beamed with enthusiasm as she talked about the musical. She didn't meet Tallulah until their first day in high school three years ago and they barely talked, even though they were on the cheerleading squad together. Stella felt bad for never reaching out to Tallulah before today but was happy she was the only person to stay behind while the others walked away. "The musical was a deciding factor on quitting cheerleading. I want to give my best performance, and I knew I couldn't do that if I was too busy with cheer and rehearsals."

"I wish I could have tried out for the musical," Tallulah said.

"Why didn't you?" Stella asked.

"Me?" Tallulah laughed. "You see how I am cheerleading. I hide behind the other girls because I don't like being the center of attention. I get nervous when there are too many people watching me. How would I be able to perform on stage?"

"I'm serious. You could've tried out to be in the chorus. That's what I did the past two years because I was just like you, too nervous to try for the lead. The only reason why I took a chance was that *Grease* is my favorite musical. I'm still in shock that I got the part."

"I wasn't shocked when I heard the news. You are very talented," Tallulah said. "Me? I can't sing and I doubt I would be able to do any of those dances in the musical."

Stella could tell how badly Tallulah wished she could've been part of the musical and tried to think of a way her friend could get involved. "Wait! I think I've got it."

"Got what?"

"How you could be part of the production."

"Stella, I already told you, I don't have the talent or confidence you have."

"No, I mean there's another way you can be part of it. It's not all about acting or singing. The drama club could always use people working in the background of the production. You could work on the sets and backstage during the actual performances," Stella suggested.

"Are you sure? Don't they already have all the people they need for it?" Tallulah asked.

"The only people Mr. Phelps has for the production are those of us with the parts. If I remember correctly, he said he could still use people to work on the sets. We need people to help paint the scenery. Come." Stella got up and took her friend's hand. "Let's go."

"Go where?" Tallulah finished the last bit of her lunch as Stella pulled her away from the table.

"We're going to the drama department and asking Mr. Phelps if you can join the production staff of the musical." Stella smiled.

Chapter Six

Another school week began, and Jake was still trying to adjust to life in a new school. He was hoping to run into Stella again, though he knew nothing could ever come of it. She was a cheerleader, and he was a regular student, a new one to make it worse. What would the school's head cheerleader see in him?

"Jake?" Jasper, his younger brother tapped on his arm. "Jake!"

"Sorry." Jake shook his head, not realizing his mind had drifted off. Jake offered to pick up Jasper from school today due to his parents staying late at work and he was helping Jasper with his homework. Having an autistic brother was the main reason Jake was impressed by Stella sticking up for Sam. From what Jake observed, Sam was non-verbal while Jasper talked to those he knew. Jake knew his brother had a hard time in school and he could only imagine how hard high school must've been for Sam.

He looked down and saw his brother was waiting for an answer. "I'm sorry, Jasper. What were you saying?"

"I was trying to tell you that I'm done with my homework. When are Mom and Dad getting home? I'm ready for dinner."

Jake looked at the time on his phone. **Six o'clock.** Jasper asked a good question. He knew his parents were going to be later than usual, but he thought they would be home by now. "Soon."

"How soon?" Jasper asked.

"I don't know." Jake sighed. "I'm hungry too. I don't know why they're so late. I bet they ran into traffic."

"I wish they would come home already." Jasper frowned.

"So do I," Jake said. He didn't know how to cook; otherwise, he would get dinner started for his brother. "Want to go look for some snacks before they come home?"

Jake was about to go into the kitchen when the front door opened and in walked his parents, Ashley and Murray. "Sorry, we're late." Ashley hugged her sons. "My car broke down and I had to call your father to come get me. I'm going to get dinner started."

"Perfect timing. I was about to go grab snacks for us. Jasper was getting hungry. Oh, and I did his homework with him, so he's all finished with it," Jake informed his parents.

"Thank you so much, Son," Murray said. "Why don't the two of you get ready for dinner?"

"Come on, Jasper." Jake brought his brother upstairs for them to get ready. A half-hour later, the family was sitting around the dinner table.

"Jake, I feel like we've been so busy the past week, we haven't asked you how school has been going?" Ashley started the conversation. This was something the family did at every dinner, discussing their days. Jake thought it was odd his parents hadn't asked since his first day at school, but he didn't want to bring it up.

"It's going better than I expected," Jake said. "I was afraid, starting in senior year and all, but I'm not being bullied. That's a first." He nervously laughed. The family moved too many times for Jake's liking and each time he started a new school, he was always bullied. He was happy when his father announced this was the final move they were ever going to make and that his job in this town was permanent. Jake was ecstatic to know he was ever going to have to adjust to a new school again.

"That's really good to hear." Ashley smiled. "And if I remember correctly, you made a new friend on your first day there."

"I did. Henry. And at the game last weekend, he introduced me to Patrick and David. Luckily for the four of us, we have lunch together. And I'm thinking of joining the drama club."

"Really?" Murray was surprised to hear his son, who never wanted to join school clubs, was interested in drama. "You want to be in the school play?"

"Dad, when have you known me to want to act in a school production?" Jake laughed. "Henry is part of behind the scenes in the drama club and they need people to help with painting and to work backstage. I know it's something I've never done before, but I do want to explore new things this year. It's alright if I join, right? I know I promised to be around for Jasper for the days you won't be able to pick him up from school."

"Son, we want you to explore new things. Plus, adding extracurricular activities will look good on your application to colleges," Ashley said.

"And drama club is one of the best clubs you can join," Murray added. "You have fun and enjoy yourself."

"Thanks," Jake said. Jasper then went on to talk about how things were going in his new school. Jake tried to listen to his brother's stories, but his mind went back to what happened in the cafeteria last week. He left out the bullying he'd witnessed, not wanting to alarm his parents.

Jake had his share of being bullied in the previous schools he'd attended once his so-called friends discovered he had an autistic brother. The one reason he was excited about starting a new school this year was that he was sick and tired of the bullying he went through the previous years. His friendship with Henry, Patrick, and David was still new and even though he didn't see them as bullies, he didn't want to take any chances.

His phone rang at the table, and he quickly read the text. "Sorry," he said. His family had a rule of no calls or texts during dinner. "It's a text from Henry asking if I want to meet up with him and the guys after dinner."

"Why don't you ask them if they'd like to come over?" Ashley suggested. "We have plenty of snacks here."

Jake's heart raced as he tried to think of a way to get out of it. He wasn't ready for his friends to meet Jasper. "Mom, I'm sure they would love that. And maybe another time I will invite them over. But Henry said they're meeting at the arcade." He quickly made up a place. "They're probably on their way over there by now."

"Alright, Son. You go and have fun. Your homework is finished, right?" Ashley asked.

"Yes. I got most of it done during my study period. I finished the rest when I got home." Jake got up and cleaned his dishes before grabbing his car keys off the counter. "I'll be back later."

He rushed out of his house before his parents could ask any more questions. He hated lying to them, but they didn't understand what was going on in his mind.

Jake drove to the park where his friends were already waiting for him to arrive. "Hey!" Henry walked up and greeted him. "We thought you may have gotten lost. It was after I told you where to meet us I realized you may not have known how to get here."

"Finding the park was no problem. I was finishing dinner when you texted me. So, what's going on?"

"The three of us were talking before you got here that we should show you around town," Henry said. "When did you move here?"

"June. But I was so nervous about starting school, I never got to explore the area," Jake said.

"Perfect! That means you don't know all the hot spots where we hang out," Patrick said.

Henry and David laughed. "Don't listen to Patrick. We don't really hang out at many places besides the park and the movie theater. We'll walk by so you know where it is.

And after, we'll head over to my place. That is where we actually do our hanging out," Henry explained.

"Sounds good to me," Jake said. The four of them left their cars by the park and started walking around the main street in town, Henry pointing out the famous joints where the high school students frequently visited. Jake was quiet as he followed, happy to have a group of friends.

Chapter Seven

Stella dreaded the next day of school after what happened at lunch the day before. Chelsea, Jodie, and Katie tried calling her during the night, phone calls she ignored. The voicemails they left all said the same thing, how she needed to rethink everything she'd said. *That's never going to happen,* she thought, getting ready for school in the morning. She was going to try her best to avoid them. Unfortunately, when she arrived at school, she saw them waiting for her at her locker. *Great.* She rolled her eyes. She forced a smile as she greeted them. "Hey."

"Stella!" Chelsea hugged her. "We need to have a talk."

"If this has anything to do with the messages you left me last night, there's no point. There is nothing left for me to say. I've made my decision," she said. She saw Tallulah standing by her locker and gave her a smile.

"Come on," Chelsea begged. "We get it. You were upset when you saw Brian being a bully. But that's in the past. You can't break up with him over one little thing."

"One little thing?" Stella had to laugh. "He was tormenting that kid. That isn't a little thing. That is a major problem. And I will not be the girlfriend of someone who sees nothing wrong with his actions. And I don't think I can be friends with people who think it was fine." She opened her locker and grabbed her books for class.

"Can you promise to just consider making up with him?" Chelsea said. "He was heartbroken when we talked to him yesterday."

"Heartbroken? Right, I'm sure he was," Stella said.

"He wants you back," Katie said.

"Did he tell you those words exactly?" Stella slammed her locker shut and turned to the girls.

"Well…" Katie began and Stella knew they were lying.

"What she means is, he didn't tell us because he didn't have to," Chelsea said. "His eyes said it all. There was hurt in those eyes. He knows he did wrong."

"So, you're telling me Brian is no longer a bully? And he won't pick on any of the students?" The girls were silent. "That's what I thought. You tell Brian, it's never going to happen. And while you're at it, tell him I wish I'd never agreed to be his girlfriend in the first place."

Chelsea reached into her purse and pulled out a letter. "We will not tell him any of that. But can you promise me one thing? That you'll read this." She handed Stella the letter.

"What is this?"

"Brian gave it to me yesterday and asked me to give it to you. It's his way of fighting for you."

Stella knew she never should've opened the letter. The

best thing to do would've been to walk away from the group and throw it in the garbage. The girls bombarding her with pleas on taking Brian back had her not thinking clearly, and she opened the note.

Stella,

I won't hold it against you for making the insane decision to break up with me. I get it. You had so much going on with cheerleading and the play, you didn't know what you were saying. And I know you didn't mean to confront me in the cafeteria. That wasn't like you at all. I am willing to put it all in the past and forget what you did if you take me back. We can make this work out.

-Brian

Stella couldn't believe it as she read the letter a couple of times. Did Brian really expect her to take him back by reading this letter when he continued to put the blame on her? He was the reason she broke up with him and this reinforced that she did the right thing. She looked at her "friends" and saw they were all waiting for a response. There was a look of hope in their faces that the letter swayed her decision. She smiled and tore the letter up.

"Since Brian has you doing his dirty work, relay this message back to him. I will never take him back. He lacks empathy for others, and I don't want to be associated with him. And when he asks what I did with the letter, you tell him exactly what I did." She handed the pieces of paper to Chelsea. "Show him this if he doesn't believe you that I tore it up."

The look on their faces was the satisfaction Stella needed to know she'd gotten her point across. She walked over to

Tallulah. "Let's go. Jake is over there with his friends," she said, ignoring her ex-friends.

"Jake?" Tallulah was confused.

"He's a new student in the school. I met him on the first day. He stopped me because he wanted to thank me for sticking up for Sam. He's the only other person, besides you, that told me I did the right thing." Stella headed over towards Jake and his friends, Tallulah following behind.

"Hi, Jake," Stella said when they reached the group of boys.

"Stella!" Jake jumped. He and his friends watched the scene with Stella and her friends play out. He hadn't realized she'd came over.

"I guess you saw what happened?"

Jake nodded. "It was hard not to watch. We overheard your friends talking before you got here about how they were going to do whatever they had to for you to take Brian back."

"You mean, my ex-friends?" Stella laughed.

"Did you really break up with him because of the bullying incident?" Jake asked.

"I did. I can't stand bullies and there was no way I was going to keep dating one." She noticed Jake's friends staring at Tallulah. "Where is my head? Let me introduce you to my friend, Tallulah."

"Hi, Tallulah," Henry said. "Are you new to this school? I don't think I've ever seen you before."

"No, I've been here for three years. But I don't really speak to anyone." Tallulah shied away.

"Tallulah is also a cheerleader." Stella was building her friend up.

"Was," Tallulah corrected her. "I quit the squad because I don't fit in with those girls. Plus, no one seemed to notice I was a cheerleader so I'm no loss to them." She laughed.

"So, what's going on with you guys?" Stella asked. She needed to change the subject, not wanting to talk about the other girls anymore.

"I was planning a movie night at my house this Saturday night. Tell you what. How about the two of you join us?" Henry asked.

"I don't know," Stella said. Something told her that this get-together was for a guys' night, and she didn't want to be a bother, and she knew Tallulah felt the same way. "I don't think either of us wants to impose," she said, and Tallulah nodded in agreement. "I'm sure you don't want us two girls ruining the night."

"You wouldn't be ruining anything. And it'll be fun to have you two there," Henry said.

Stella looked at Tallulah. "Well, we do have plenty of free time now that we aren't doing cheerleading anymore."

"I don't know," Tallulah's voice was quiet. "You know I'm shy when talking to people I don't know."

"You won't be alone. I'll be there." Stella smiled. She turned back to Henry. "We'll be there."

"Perfect," Henry said. "One four nine six Parrish Avenue. Do you need directions?" He wrote his address down for Stella.

"I know where the street is. Thank you. And I'm sure

we'll see each other in the halls before then." Stella turned her attention to Jake and smiled. "See you around."

Jake waited until Stella and Tallulah walked away when he turned to his friend. "Did you just invite Stella to the movie night?"

"I did."

"And she did say yes, right? I didn't imagine her saying she'll be there. Did I?"

"No, you didn't." Henry laughed. "Why do you sound so surprised by it?"

"I guess I'm just in shock that the head cheerleader agreed to come to a movie night we're having. We're not even the type of guys she associates with," Jake said.

"Didn't you hear what she said? She and Tallulah are no longer on the cheerleading squad," Henry said.

"I was in such shock that you asked her, I wasn't paying attention. She actually said that?"

"She did. Plus, I did hear the news yesterday after school that she went to the moderator and quit. That's what made me ask her to come over. Also, her friend does seem nice. Can't believe I never noticed her in school before."

Jake knew what Henry was getting at. "She does seem nice."

"Jake, you don't mind that I invited the two of them over, do you? I know you're still trying to adjust to living here and it was supposed to be a guys' night. But I didn't think there would be a problem inviting the two of them to join us."

Do I mind? Of course, I don't mind! You've given me a way to get to know Stella better! Jake's mind screamed. He couldn't tell this to his friend. He hardly knew Stella, other than she was willing to help students in need. "I don't mind at all. The more the merrier. Right?"

"Now you're thinking! It'll be fun." Henry patted Jake on the back.

"It sure will be." Jake smiled. "I better head to class if I want to make it before the bell rings. I'll see you at lunch."

Jake had more than enough time to get to class, but he wanted to be on his own. He couldn't believe how events were starting to play out in his life. He knew he had a crush on Stella. It happened the moment he met her in the hall last week. But when Henry told him she was dating the star football player, Jake knew he never stood a chance.

This past weekend, everything began to change. He was hanging out with Henry, David, and Patrick more. And now, he was going to be having a movie night with Stella. Granted, the others were going to be there, but this allowed Jake to talk to Stella outside of school. And he couldn't wait.

He did feel a little guilty for hiding Jasper from his friends, especially since he would be getting closer to Stella this weekend. He didn't want to begin their friendship with a lie, but he still needed to see how others would react before he told them about Jasper. *I can do this. I just can't let anything slip out before I'm ready to tell them,* Jake told himself as he walked into the classroom. He knew it was going to be hard to concentrate in today's classes.

Chapter Eight

Sunday morning, Stella woke up smiling. She had an amazing time at Henry's the night before. Movie night turned out to be three movies before everyone decided it was getting late and time to go home. After dropping Tallulah off at home, Stella returned to her house feeling the best she had all week. Her parents were happy to see their daughter was feeling better and no longer thinking about Brian.

Stella's phone buzzed on her nightstand as she yawned. She reached across and saw a text from Tallulah.

Tallulah: Had a great time last night. Henry texted me asking if we'd like to meet up at the mall this afternoon and go bowling. Want to go?

Stella was excited. After last night, she wouldn't mind hanging out with Jake and his friends again. She never had as much fun as she had the night before when she hung out with the cheerleaders.

Stella: Count me in. I just have to get ready and then I'll head on out.

Even though they wouldn't be meeting with the boys until the afternoon, Stella always liked to be early. She got ready for the day, putting on a sapphire sundress and royal blue sandals. She put her hair up into a ponytail and made her way downstairs, grabbing a quick breakfast.

"You're dressed up for a Sunday," Darlene said when she noticed her daughter in the kitchen.

"Tallulah texted me that Henry wants us to all meet at the mall this afternoon. I'm going to head over after breakfast. Maybe I can do some shopping before we go bowling."

"Now, who's Henry again?" James asked his daughter.

"Jake's friend. And if you ask me, I think he's got a little crush on Tallulah." She smiled.

"And Jake is…" James asked, not recognizing the name.

"Oh, I never told you about Jake. I met him on the first day of school. He came over to tell me I was brave to stand up to Brian. He's new to our school, so I'm trying to make him feel welcome."

"That's wonderful," Darlene said. "Have fun at the mall."

Stella finished breakfast and headed to the mall. After parking her car, she grabbed her phone from her purse and texted Tallulah.

Stella: At the mall. Wanted to do some shopping before everyone arrives. I'll see you soon.

The rest of the kids showed up around noon and they met in the food court. Henry joined everyone with passes in his hand. "Alright, I got us all down for a game of bowling.

The bowling alley here is glow-in-the-dark, so I wanted to make sure I got lanes for us to play before they're all booked. Let's get something to eat first and then we can head over. I got two lanes for us, and they'll be free at one-thirty."

Stella took her pass and walked off with Tallulah to grab a burrito while the boys opted for fast food. "This is fun, isn't it?" Stella said as they waited for their order.

"I don't know why I said I would come." Tallulah was nervous. "I don't know how to bowl. Not well, at least. I've only gone a few times with my family. Never with friends before."

"You have nothing to worry about. Remember when we agreed to go to Henry's yesterday, and you were nervous? What went wrong when we were there?"

"Nothing," Tallulah answered.

"Exactly." Stella smiled. "And nothing will go wrong. We're all friends here and no one is going to make fun of us for not being good at bowling."

The girls got their burritos and found the boys sitting at a table. "Over here!" Jake waved Stella and Tallulah over. "I'm glad you decided to come," Jake said to Stella when she took a seat.

"Well, thank you for the invite." Stella smiled. "If Tallulah hadn't texted me this morning telling me, I would've been bored at home."

"Have you guys done the bowling here?" Henry asked. "I heard it's so much fun."

"I heard from other friends that it's better than regular bowling," Stella said. She laughed at her own comment when she realized it was Chelsea who'd told her about the glow-in-the-dark bowling. "But I've never done it."

"Guess it'll be a learning experience for all of us," Jake said.

"See. What was I telling you?" Stella whispered to Tallulah. "You have nothing to worry about. All of us are going to be equally bad at this." She laughed.

They all enjoyed their lunch, laughing and telling stories. Jake told about his life before moving to this town and how his father's job brought him to different towns. "Out of all the schools I've been to, this is my favorite one." He looked at Stella when he said those words.

Stella blushed at Jake's glimpse and Henry knew it was time to get things moving. "Alright, then." He got up from his seat. "We should start heading over to the bowling alley."

The five had a great time bowling, Stella and Tallulah winning in the end. Stella didn't say anything to Tallulah, but she had a feeling the boys let them win. Either way, it was all in good fun.

"Stella, know what I realized?" Tallulah went up to Stella as they returned their bowling shoes.

"That we were worried for nothing about thinking we were going to be horrible at this?" Stella laughed.

"Well, that too. While we were playing, I was thinking of how much fun we had last night at Henry's, and it dawned on me. We had a better time with them than we would've if we had gone to the party Friday night."

"You know, I was thinking the same thing. I've never been to one of those football parties and I know I wouldn't have enjoyed myself if I went. What would I have done? Sat on the couch, ignoring everyone. Well, they would ignore me first. And I don't think I would've been welcomed there after dumping Brian. Or even worse, he would've been the only guy bothering me, trying to get me to take him back." Stella shuddered at the thought.

"Maybe you'll be lucky, and he got a new girlfriend at the party," Tallulah said.

"I really hope so. I don't know how much more I can deal with him trying to get me to take him back." Stella rolled her eyes.

"Hey!" Henry called out to the girls. "Ready to go? We were thinking of getting ice cream before heading home."

Stella looked at Tallulah and giggled. "Let's go!" she said as they followed the boys to the ice cream shop in the mall.

J ake was in the living room watching television with his family but wasn't paying attention to the show. He was thinking back to how much fun he'd had today at the mall. He tried his best not to keep staring at Stella, but he couldn't help it. She was so beautiful, and he'd never met a girl quite like her before. Jake hated when they all parted ways after a great afternoon at the mall, but they'd promised to do this more often.

Jasper got up from his seat in the living room and walked over to Jake on the couch and pulled him into a tight hug, surprising Jake.

"What was that for?" Jake asked, hugging his brother back.

"Just wanted to give you a hug. Jake, why were you smiling just now?"

"Was I smiling?" Jake hadn't noticed.

"Yes. And there wasn't anything funny on television either."

"Oh, I wasn't smiling because of what we're watching. I was smiling because I was thinking what a great time I had with my friends today," Jake explained.

"What did you guys do?" Jasper asked.

"We went to the bowling alley in the mall. You know what? I should take you there one weekend," Jake told his brother. "The alley is glow-in-the-dark, nothing like the bowling alleys we went to in the last town we lived in. You'll have so much fun. Would you like to do that?"

"YES!" Jasper screamed in excitement, and he turned to his parents. "I can go with Jake, right?"

"Yes, Jasper." Ashley smiled. "We'll pick a week when we can all go as a family."

Excited, Jasper hugged his brother and rushed upstairs to his room. "That was really a nice idea, Jake," Murray said. "Not many boys your age would want to hang out with their little brother."

"While I was bowling with my friends today, the first thing I thought was, Jasper would love this. And you both know how much I love to spend time with him. I may be leaving next year for college. Though, I have a feeling I won't be going to a college far away." Jake laughed.

"Wherever you decide to go to college, all that matters is it has the program you want." Murray smiled.

"So, tell us, how was it at the mall?" Ashley changed the subject. "You did come home the happiest I've seen you for a very long time."

"If you ask me, I think our son may have a crush on a girl," Murray said. "I'm right, aren't I?"

"Maybe." Jake blushed. "Her name is Stella. She was the head cheerleader until this week. Long story." He nervously laughed. "I met her on the first day of school. She was at Henry's house last night for the movie night. I had no idea Henry invited her to the mall today until I got there."

"I was right, he does have a crush," Murray said.

"Alright, you got me." Jake laughed. "When I met her, I was afraid nothing could come of it. She was head cheerleading and dating the school's football star."

"And she's not anymore?" his father asked.

Jake shook his head. "Her ex was bullying an autistic student and Stella stood up to him. I don't know the whole story of her breaking up with him or quitting cheerleading, but she did. I want to ask her out, but I'm giving her time since she just broke up with the guy. As long as Henry keeps inviting her and her friend to hang out with us, it gives me time to get to know her better. And I'll take that for the time being."

"Jake, you have no idea how happy we are that this school year is going better for you than the ones you've attended in the past," Ashley said.

"Your mother is right. We were worried you were going to be bullied again," Murray said.

"What can I say? I'm lucky I became friends with Henry on the first day of school." Jake swallowed hard. His parents had no idea why he wasn't being bullied this year. The other schools he attended had students who bullied him because of Jasper. And that was why he didn't let anyone know he had an autistic brother. He didn't want to go through another school year like he did last year.

"That's really good to hear," Ashley said. "Your father and I were so worried this year wasn't going to be easy for you."

"I was afraid of that, too," Jake admitted. "Henry was the first student to come up to me when I walked into the school. At first, I thought he was a student forced to show me around and he wouldn't want to be friends with the new kid in school. But then he told me he saw I looked lost and offered to show me around. Before I knew it, we were making plans to hang out at lunch. I never had a best friend before, especially with all the moving we've done. It's nice to finally have one." Jake smiled.

"Jake, I just thought of something," Ashley said. "Why don't you invite Henry to come over next weekend?"

"Next weekend?" Jake's heart pounded. He still wasn't ready for Henry, or any of his other new friends, to meet his family. "I think we already planned to have another movie night at his house."

"You can always have it here," Murray suggested. "We wouldn't mind."

Quick! Think of an excuse! Jake's mind screamed. He had to get out of this without his parents figuring out the truth. "I like the idea, but Henry has a better television to watch movies." It wasn't a lie. Henry's television had surround sound, it made you feel as if you were in a movie theater. "But I'll let him know the offer so we can pick another day." Jake got up off the couch. He knew he was never going to tell Henry his parents wanted him to come over so they could meet him. "I'm going to head up to my room. I'm tired from the day."

"Yes, of course. You better get your sleep for school tomorrow," Murray said.

Jake said goodnight to his parents before going to Jasper's room and saying goodnight to his brother. Sadly, he walked to his bedroom and closed the door. Every time he saw his brother, he hated he was hiding Jasper from his friends. He'd finally found a school he enjoyed going to and friends he didn't want to lose. Until he felt ready, he couldn't let the truth out.

Chapter Nine

Stella put all her time and effort into the play over the next week. She'd finally talked Tallulah into joining the production crew and on most days, the two of them spent after school working on the sets. Stella knew once rehearsals started, she wouldn't have time to work behind the scenes. She wanted to get as much work done now to help out Mr. Phelps and the rest of the production crew.

They were busy painting in the drama department when there was a knock on the door. "Who could that be?" Tallulah asked. She and Stella were alone working on the sets today and weren't expecting anyone to visit.

"I don't know." Stella got up and went to open the door. "Jake! Henry! What are you doing here?" When Stella and Tallulah weren't busy at the drama department, they were spending their time hanging out with Jake and Henry. But neither showed an interest in the school musical.

"Yesterday, when you were talking about how much fun you two were having working on the sets, it had us thinking we should join," Henry explained. "That is if we are allowed to. We never joined the drama club."

"Yes, we could definitely use the help. You don't need to be in the drama club to help out." She welcomed them into the room. "Tallulah, look who's here to help us out!" Stella was excited.

"Henry!" Tallulah found it hard to hide her enthusiasm. "And Jake! You really want to help us out?"

"Yes. I hope you don't mind." Henry smiled.

"No. We don't mind at all." Tallulah blushed.

"Is it just the two of you?" Jake asked when he saw no one was around.

"Yeah." Stella sighed. "I don't know where everyone is. So many people signed up to work behind the scenes, but when it comes to actually doing the work, no one is around when we need them. Technically, I shouldn't even be working behind the scenes since I'm in the play, but I told Mr. Phelps I'd help until rehearsals start. Then, that's all I'll be concentrating on."

"So, what are the two of you doing today?" Jake asked, walking over to where Henry now stood with Tallulah by the finished sets.

"Well, we're starting with the sets we need for the first few scenes, which are the school building and classrooms. The artists already drew the sets and all we're doing is filling it in with the paint." Stella showed Jake.

"These are amazing." Jake admired the work. Whoever the artists were that did the sketches for the scenes are talented. "The drama club means a lot to you, doesn't it?" he asked Stella.

"For as long as I can remember, I've always wanted to be a part of it once I started high school. Unfortunately, this will be the last year of the club." Stella looked down at the floor.

"What do you mean?" Tallulah asked. "For you, but others will do a play next year?"

"That's how it's always been up until now."

"But? I feel there's a but in there," Jake said.

"There is." Stella took a deep breath. She hated being the one to bring the bad news. "Mr. Phelps told us this is his last year at the school."

"I can't say I'm surprised he's retiring. He was the drama teacher when my older brother was here years ago," Henry said. "But what does that have to do with the drama club? I'm sure another teacher could take over."

"That's what I thought, but then Mr. Phelps told us that for the past few years, the department has been struggling. Why do you think they're asking for students to work on the scenery this year? They usually hire professionals to do this kind of work. The school no longer has money in the budget to keep putting on productions every year. Mr. Phelps has been fighting every year for the administration to keep it happening, but they finally decided to put an end to the drama department. They're claiming there's no point in keeping it when no one is interested in the musicals."

"They don't know what they're talking about," Tallulah said. "Every year I can't wait for the productions. And now, just like that, they're going to put an end to it?"

"I'm afraid so," Stella said. "Mr. Phelps said if they were going to get rid of the drama department, then he's leaving.

Guess they didn't care and they're letting him retire a few years before he planned to. Now, I've been talking to the other cast members, many of us have been working with Mr. Phelps since freshman year, and we've all decided that we want to make this the best send-off for him. And we're going to chip in and find a special present to give him after the last show."

Jake stood aside as he listened to Stella talk. She wasn't crying, but Jake could tell she was holding back tears. He didn't know Stella for long, but he could tell the drama club was important to her and how this news broke her heart. He wished there was something he could do to make her feel better. *Maybe there is something I can do*. He smiled.

"Stella, does it have to only be cast members to chip in for the present?" he asked.

"Well, we never discussed anyone else being a part of it, but I don't think that will be a problem. Why?"

"I was just thinking. Henry said Mr. Phelps has been a part of this school for a long time. What are we talking about? Decades? What if we send word out to the students about the idea of sending him off with a blast? Have them donate as much as they want to, especially those who know and love him. I don't have him as a teacher and even I want to donate money towards his gift. I'm sure others would feel the same way." Jake waited for Stella to respond, hoping his idea didn't sound ridiculous.

"Jake! That is a wonderful idea!" Stella grabbed Jake into an embrace. "I never thought about getting the rest of the school involved. You're right, I'm sure many would donate. And it'll show the administration how loved he is to so many students." She pulled away from the hug and grabbed her phone. "I'm going to text the others and let them know."

"I'm glad I could help." Jake smiled. He watched as Stella excitedly texted her friends and saw a change in her attitude from when she was telling them the news. The hug she gave him meant the world, though Jake knew it was nothing more than a friendly gesture. *Baby steps,* he reminded himself. *She only broke up a couple weeks ago with her boyfriend.*

He walked over to where Henry was painting a set and went to help. Jake was willing to participate in any event if it meant getting close to Stella.

Chapter Ten

"Hi, I'm Stella Eaves. I was told to come here. A Damien Shield is expecting me," Stella told the young man she met at the front desk of Ability Sports Club. During the week she received a call from Damien Shield, volunteer coordinator of the club telling her he got her name from the volunteer list at the library. Every Saturday morning, the club was open for people with special needs, and they needed more volunteers. Stella had been waiting for a call like this and she didn't hesitate to tell Damien that she was excited to start volunteer work at the club.

"Stella Eaves," the man repeated her name and looked down at a list. "Yes, I see your name right here. Damien is busy right now, but you'll be able to talk to him during the morning when he comes into the activity room. I'm John Carlson, a volunteer here. Damien has you scheduled to work with kids in the activity room." John got up from his desk and showed her a room down the hall. "The room straight down the hall is where you'll be."

"Thank you," Stella said and headed in the direction of the room. She was apprehensive from the moment she woke up this morning, not knowing what to expect. After meeting John, she started to feel a little more confident. *I wonder if all the volunteers are as friendly and helpful as he is,* she thought, opening the door and walking into the activity room.

"Hi!" A girl around Stella's age greeted her. "I'm Debbie."

"Hi. I'm Stella. I'm a new volunteer."

"Oh, yes, Damien told me you would be coming today. I can't thank you enough for signing up to be a volunteer. We could always use more, especially on Saturday mornings. Let me take a look and see what station we could use you at today."

"Thank you." Stella stepped aside to look around the room. She couldn't wait to get started. She was amazed to see a variety of ages here. One side of the room was for children and the other side was for adults.

"Stella, come with me," Debbie said. "We could use you at the polybat station for the first hour. It's mostly older kids here during this time. After, come back to me and I'll have you work with some of the younger children who come in. And today there's going to be more than usual coming in. Damien is having an open house for anyone who wants to check out the special program we have on Saturday mornings," she explained to Stella as she showed her to the polybat station.

Stella was excited to be at the polybat station as it was one of her favorite games. It was similar to table tennis, and she played it all the time with her brothers. She took in her surroundings as she made her way to the station, amazed to see how many different things the club offered to the people here today.

"There are a lot of stations here," she said to Debbie.

"One thing Damien wanted when he started this program was a variety for children to choose from. We know these kids have different special needs and there are some events they may be more comfortable with than others."

"When did this program start, if you don't mind me asking?"

"Ten years ago, I think. I started volunteering here last year." Debbie stopped at the station Stella was going to be helping at. "I'm really glad there's another high school student volunteering here. Before you came today, I was the only one."

"I feel that it's important for people our age to help out." Stella smiled.

"That's great to hear. Have fun and I'll be in the front of the room if you have any questions. I'll be back in an hour to take you to the other station where you'll be with the younger kids."

Stella was having fun with the kids at the polybat station, playing with them. The smiles on their faces were all she needed to see to know they were having a good time. It didn't take her long to discover the polybat station was popular among the kids who were there. Across from her station was the archery station. And judging from the line that formed from the station, it was just as popular.

After half an hour, the line at the polybat station died

down and Stella walked over to have a look at the archery station. The woman who was helping at the location walked over to Stella. "Hi, you must be new here. I'm Christine McCormick and that's my husband, Rodney."

"Hi, I'm Stella. I just started today. I see this station is very popular. Many of the kids came here after playing polybat with me."

"It's always been that way." Christine laughed and Rodney joined them. "Rodney, this is Stella, she just started volunteering today," she introduced Stella to her husband.

"It's a pleasure to meet you, Stella." Rodney shook her hand. "Wow, they gave you one of the popular stations on your first day. That's impressive." He smiled. "It's good to see another teenager here, giving up their Saturday morning to help out. We could use more like you here."

"Have you two been volunteering for long?" Stella asked.

"Ten years. We were the first ones to volunteer when Damien started the program. Not many stay here for long as things come up, but we make sure to come here every Saturday," Christine explained.

"When we saw some of the kids were having trouble using the equipment we had here based on their needs, Christine and I developed equipment to better suit them. That is what you see here." He pointed to the items at their station. "We have a variety for the kids to choose from, that way no kid is left out."

"This really is amazing," Stella said. "The kids are lucky to have people like you volunteering here."

"Every person who volunteers here is a hero to the kids

who come here," Rodney said. "Notice how on the other side of the room there are adults? When Damien saw how popular the club was for kids, he expanded it for adults to be welcomed on Saturdays."

Stella listened in amazement as Rodney and Christine gave her all the information she needed about being a volunteer at the club and she was glad to be here. Debbie walked over to where the three were talking and pulled Stella aside.

"Sorry to interrupt you, but Stella I could use you at the other station. We have a child who is here for the first time and he's a little nervous. I'm sure you will be able to help him," Debbie said.

"Sure. Where is he?"

Debbie brought Stella into another section of the room where a young boy with piercing blue eyes was sitting alone in the corner. "His name is Jasper. His mother had to leave to take care of some errands, and he ran to the corner and won't come out. I tried to get him to play with some of the other kids his age, but he wants to stay alone. Maybe you can find out what it is he likes to do for fun and we can find the perfect station for him."

"I'm on it." Stella smiled and headed towards Jasper. She noticed he was reading a book he'd brought with him. "What do you have over here?" she asked, sitting next to him on the floor. Jasper didn't lift his head from his book, ignoring Stella's presence. "Jasper, is it?" Stella tried again, but the young boy refused to talk. Stella was determined to get through to him. "So, they told me it's your first day here. Want to know a little secret? It's my first day here too. And I was just as nervous when I walked through those doors. I've volunteered at many places before, but never here. Jasper, it's alright to be nervous. I'm here to help."

Jasper remained quiet, but Stella remained patient. She didn't know what special needs group Jasper was a part of, but she didn't want him to feel as if he wasn't wanted here. "Tell you what. Why don't I take you to the station I was helping at? Do you want to play polybat? That sounds like fun, doesn't it?"

Annoyed by Stella's persistence, Jasper put his book back in his backpack and got up, walking away. Stella sighed, feeling as if she didn't accomplish anything. She walked over to Debbie. "I tried with that kid, but he didn't speak to me. Just got up and walked away."

Debbie shook her head. "I was afraid that would happen. His mother said he has autism."

"I wonder if he has the same kind as a kid in my school. He isn't verbal and communicated with me through an AAC device," Stella said, remembering the day she'd met Sam.

"I don't think that's it. I mean, he talked to his mother when he got here. It was once she said she was dropping him off and coming back later he ran and hid. I think he was hoping his mother was going to stay." Debbie was silent for a few moments. "I have an idea. Why don't you talk to his mother when she comes back? Maybe she can give you some ideas of how to get through to her son."

Stella nodded and went over to a group of kids who were playing near Jasper. She kept an eye on the lonely boy as she watched the kids in the area. Not long after the incident with Jasper, Debbie came over with his mother.

"Stella, this is Jasper's mom. I told her what happened and that you would like to speak to her," Debbie introduced the two.

"Hi." Stella shook Ashley's hand. "It's nice to meet you."

"Likewise." Ashley smiled. "I am so sorry Jasper acted that way towards you. I was hoping bringing him here would be good for him. He's very talkative when he's with people he knows, but shy whenever he's with new people. That was one reason I left him here when I went running my errands. I was hoping it would break him out of that pattern. I guess I was wrong."

"I want you to know, I will not give up on your son." Stella smiled. "I will do whatever I can to get him to talk to me and from there, hopefully, he'll make friends here. What kind of music does he like?"

"He's not really into music. But he's into Marvel comic books, especially Spider-Man."

"Really. That's good to know. I'm going to ask my brothers if they have any comic books I can have to give to Jasper."

"You don't have to do that."

"I know I don't have to, but I want to," Stella said.

Damien didn't make an appearance until the two hours of the program was up. Stella was upset that the time went by quickly. She was having a great time meeting the kids and volunteers and hated seeing it come to an end. She was helping the volunteers clean up the activity room for it to be ready for the public when Damien walked over to her.

"Stella? It's great to finally meet you after only speaking to you on the phone."

"Damien, I can't thank you enough for giving me the opportunity of helping out."

"I take it that your first day went very well." Damien smiled.

"It did. And I hope I can come back to volunteer."

"Now that you mention it, I'm glad you brought that up. Debbie told me how amazing you were with the kids; I was hoping you would be able to come back next weekend."

"Yes!" Stella was a little too excited by Damien's offer. "I would love to."

"Great. We'll see you next Saturday."

Stella said goodbye to the volunteers, who were all happy to hear she would be returning the next weekend. And she was pleased that for the most part, the day went well. But she couldn't help but think of Jasper.

She couldn't wait to get home and tell her parents about her first day of volunteer work and how the coordinator wanted her to come back. She told them that today was the day she discovered what she wanted to do, to help kids who had special needs, and being a volunteer at Ability Sports Club was only the beginning. She now knew what kind of program to look for when it came to colleges.

Chapter Eleven

"Doesn't it feel great to be doing this?' Jake asked Henry. The two of them were in the drama department after school painting the next set of sets. This week, they were working on the scenery for *Greased Lightnin'* scene and Jake was having fun working behind the scenes of the musical.

"Doing what? Painting?" Henry asked, not taking his eyes off the scene he was painting. He was a perfectionist and made sure he didn't let anything distract him.

"Not just the painting. I mean helping out the drama club." Jake stopped painting to take a break. "Do you want to take a break? I could use a soda."

Henry thought about it before putting his paintbrush down. "You're right. Let's grab a soda. We're the only ones here right now. They won't mind if we take a quick break." It was odd for the two of them to be in the room alone, but Mr. Phelps told him they could get ahead before he came with the others on the production crew.

The two left the drama room, passing by the stage as

they headed towards the cafeteria. Stella was on the stage, practicing singing when Jake stopped to watch her. *She's so beautiful and talented,* Jake thought, not taking his eyes off Stella.

"Jake," Henry was calling out his friend's name, but Jake didn't hear a word he was saying. "Are we going to get the soda or not? Jake! Hey! Jake!" He grabbed his friend's arm, pulling him away from the stage, not wanting to disrupt the rehearsal.

"What is it?" Jake said once he and Henry were in the hall.

"I was calling your name when I realized I walked out without you. Then, what a surprise, you were standing there watching Stella." Henry pretended to be shocked by Jake's behavior.

"Oh, come on, I'm not that bad." Jake laughed.

"Not that bad?" Henry cracked up laughing. "Don't tell me you don't see how you get whenever Stella is around."

"She's a friend. That is all and nothing more," Jake said and headed to the cafeteria.

"Well, I already know that." Henry rolled his eyes. "This is how it's obvious you want her as something more."

The two reached the vending machines and Jake stopped and looked at Henry. "How do you know that's how I feel?"

"You just admitted it." Henry laughed. "Honestly, it's so noticeable. Every time she walks into the room, you smile."

"I do not," Jake got defensive. His friend wasn't lying, but Jake worried Stella picked up on his behavior.

"Fine, keep lying to yourself. If you ask me, I don't know

why you haven't asked her out already. She's single and you would be a much better boyfriend than Brian ever was to her."

Jake ignored Henry. He got his soda out of the machine. "Let's get our soda and get back to the drama room."

"Why? So, you can go back to watching Stella rehearse?" Henry raised his eyebrows.

"No. I want to get back so we can finish the work we were doing on the sets before Mr. Phelps comes back. So, unless you want to stay here and talk about my non-existent love life with yourself, I'm going back," Jake said heading down the hall.

"Jake, don't be like that." Henry followed him towards the drama room. "There's no reason to get so touchy. I'm only telling you what I observe whenever Stella is near you."

"Whatever. I don't want to talk about it." Jake stopped before opening the door to the room. "Great. Mr. Phelps is back, and we wasted all this time talking nonsense."

"He's back?"

"Yes, and Tallulah is with him," Jake said.

"Tallulah?" Henry's face lit up.

"Ha! Now, who's got a crush on one of our friends?" Jake laughed when Henry blushed. "You said it's obvious how I feel about Stella? Let's just say, if I were you, I wouldn't let Tallulah see how red your face is right now."

Mr. Phelps stopped talking to Tallulah when Jake and Henry walked into the room. "There you two are. I was beginning to wonder what happened when I didn't see you in here."

"Sorry about that. We decided to take a quick break and grab soda while waiting for you to come back," Jake explained. "We're just about finished with the sets we started yesterday and then we're ready for what you want us to do next."

"Alright, why don't the two of you finish your current project, and then tomorrow I'll have the new sets for you to work on," Mr. Phelps said and turned his attention back to Tallulah. "Now, as I was saying, you've been hanging around the drama department for quite some time. Have you considered joining the production?"

"Me?" Tallulah nervously laughed. "No. Plus, I thought you already have everyone you need for the play. I'm not an actress and I definitely can't dance."

"There's more to the production than just acting. We need people to join our orchestra, and I heard you are a flautist."

Tallulah shook her head. She was a flautist, but she hadn't picked up her flute in a few years, not since joining the cheerleaders. She'd only told one person about playing the flute and she knew who must've told Mr. Phelps. "Stella told you, didn't she?"

"She was hoping to get you more involved with the production and suggested it. And the one instrument we're missing is the flute."

"Mr. Phelps, thank you for considering me, but it's been about three years since I last played my flute. If I start playing it now, I'm afraid I'll be rusty."

"That won't be a problem. How long did you play before you stopped?"

"About six years," Tallulah responded.

"Know what I'll do? If you agree to join the orchestra, I'll speak to the conductor to help you brush up on your playing," Mr. Phelps said.

"Mr. Phelps, I don't know what to say. I would appreciate that so much. Will I still be able to work on painting the sets if I join the orchestra? I'm having fun doing that."

"Yes." Mr. Phelps laughed. "You, along with Jake and Henry, are the only ones I can count on to stop by every day after school to help. And now that I'm starting with rehearsals, I need all the help I can get with the behind-the-scenes stuff."

"Mr. Phelps, would it be alright if I step out for a moment? I want to call my mom and tell her the news. She's going to be thrilled to know I'm going to play the flute again. I think she's been waiting for me to start playing it again."

"Yes, of course." Mr. Phelps smiled. "It's going to be a joy having you join the production."

"Hey! Hey! Did you hear that?" Henry hit Jake's arm.

"Watch it! You're getting your paint on my clothes." He moved his friend's hand away, so the paintbrush was away from his shirt.

"Tallulah is going to be in the orchestra," Henry said, paying no attention to Jake. "And she's going to continue to help us with the sets."

Jake looked at his best friend and shook his head. "Now who's got it bad for a girl?" He put his paintbrush down and crossed his arms.

"What do you mean?"

"You were giving me crap earlier for how I act when Stella is around, yet you're acting the same way with Tallulah."

"I am not," Henry said.

"Right. I'm sure you blush like this normally." Jake laughed.

"Fine. You caught me. Yes, I have a crush on Tallulah. There. Are you happy now?" Henry said. "I admit it."

"Now, was that so hard to do?" Jake raised an eyebrow.

"No. But I don't see why you won't admit your crush on Stella."

"What are you talking about? I didn't think there was anything to admit because you said it was obvious. Plus, I'm not denying I have a crush on her. I'm just waiting for the right time to ask her out. That's all."

"Tell me one thing, Jake. When is it going to be the right time to ask her out?"

"Honestly, I don't know." Jake felt defeated. He could see how happy his best friend was having a crush on Tallulah and wasn't afraid to show it when Tallulah was around. Jake, on the other hand, was being careful not to give away his feelings for Stella. Not before she was ready to get into another relationship.

～

Saturday morning, Stella returned to the Ability Sports Club, less nervous than she was the previous week. She carried a bag with her containing Spider-Man comic books her brothers let her have, hoping Jasper would like them. She walked inside the club and headed towards the activity room after greeting John in the front lobby. Debbie was waiting for her when she arrived.

"You're here!" Debbie grabbed her into a hug. "I was so happy when I heard Damien wanted you to come back this weekend."

"I'm glad to be back." Stella smiled. She looked around, wondering if Jasper was here today. Debbie noticed the look on her face and knew exactly what was going on.

"He's right there." Debbie pointed to Jasper, once again alone in the corner. "His mother wants him to start getting used to being with other kids his age without her around. So far, it's not working. What's in the bag?" she asked, noticing the bag in Stella's hands.

"Last weekend, I asked Jasper's mother what he was interested in and she told me Marvel comic books. Luckily, my brothers are into the same comics, and they had plenty they didn't want anymore. Figured Jasper may want them." She looked at Jasper and sighed. "Hope this works and gets him to open up to me."

"That is so nice of you to do something like that. I hope it helps. I hate seeing him sitting alone," Debbie said.

"Me too. I tried to get him to play polybat last weekend, but he didn't want to. His mother said he's shy when it comes to talking to strangers. I want him to know I'm not a stranger, but someone who wants to help him and be his friend. Hopefully, I win him over with the comics." Stella laughed.

"Good luck." Debbie smiled. "And if you need any help, I'll be here. And don't worry about going to the polybat station today. Take your time with Jasper."

Stella thanked Debbie again and walked over to Jasper. "Hi, Jasper. Do you remember me? I'm Stella. We met last week." Jasper responded the same way he did last week, ignoring her and keeping his head in his book. "Ok, then. I got you a present." She put the bag of comics down in front of him. "You open it when you're ready to."

Jasper eyed Stella before reaching for the bag and taking out the comic books. A small smile spread across his face. He looked through the five books and handed her one of them. He still didn't speak to her. She took the book from him. "Do you want me to read this to you?"

Jasper nodded and sat against the wall as Stella began to read. She finished the first book when Jasper already had another one in his hand for her to read. A third comic book quickly followed.

"Jasper, how about we take a break from reading and do something else? Why don't we go play polybat? There are kids your age at that station," she suggested.

Jasper looked at her and got up, walking away and finding another corner to sit in. Stella cursed herself for pushing Jasper to do something he wasn't ready for. *I need to remember to take things slow with him. If he isn't ready to talk to me, why did I think he would be ready to play with other kids?*

She gathered the books and put them back into the bag, looking for Jasper.

She found him sitting on the far side of the room, away from everyone. She didn't want to get too close to him, in case seeing her caused him to run away again. Jasper looked up and saw her and she grabbed one of the books out of the bag as a peace offering. He smiled as she walked over and sat down next to him. She spent the rest of the morning reading the comic books to Jasper until his mother came.

Stella stayed to help the volunteers clean up the activity room once everyone left when Damien came up to her asking if they could talk. They walked to his office. "What did you want to talk about?" She worried she did something wrong.

Damien noticed the worried look on her face. "Don't worry, I didn't call you in here for anything bad. Quite the opposite." He smiled. "I don't think you saw me because you were busy, but I came into the room today and saw you reading to Jasper."

"You did?" She was so involved with getting through to Jasper, she hadn't noticed Damien was there. "I hope it was fine for me to bring comic books in for him."

"It's perfectly fine. Anything that helps the kids is what matters. I was speaking to Debbie, and she told me how Jasper wasn't communicating with anyone. I was getting worried this might not be the right program for him, but when I saw you reading to him, I knew he was meant to be here with us. Debbie said how he warmed up to you once you showed him the comic books. I'm impressed with how quickly you were able to get through to him. I've seen children like him who have taken months to start feeling comfortable with our volunteers. And with you, it only took a week."

"Before signing up to volunteer, I read up on autism and after speaking to Jasper's mother last weekend, I tried to think of the best way to get him to respond to me. He still doesn't talk to me, but he's letting me sit with him. That's a start." Stella smiled. "I'll continue to take baby steps with him until he's completely comfortable with me and the kids here. I made the mistake of trying to get him to play with them today. But now I know he isn't ready."

"You're doing an amazing job and I'm grateful to have you as a volunteer. See you next weekend." Damien smiled.

Stella smiled and left his office. She said goodbye to the other volunteers before heading out to her car. She couldn't wait to get home and tell her parents about today.

Chapter Twelve

Next Saturday, Jake sat in the kitchen with Jasper, eating breakfast, when their mother walked into the kitchen. "Jasper, have you told Jake about the club you go to on Saturdays?" she asked. Jasper shook his head and continued eating his breakfast. "Why don't you tell him? I'm sure he would love to hear about it."

Jasper finished eating his cereal. "It's at the sports club in town."

"So, that's where you've been going every Saturday. Is it fun?" Jake asked.

Jasper shrugged. "There are all these activities there, but they aren't for me. I sit and read."

Ashley looked at Jake. "I'm hoping this place would bring him out of his shyness, but he likes to be alone once he gets there. The girl who volunteers there gave him comic books. Last week, he stayed with her as she read them to her. I'm happy he finally let her do that, but I wish he would play with kids his age."

Jake turned to his brother. "Jasper, why don't you want to do any of the sports? You love when we play together."

"That's because I'm playing with you. I don't know the kids there. And it's different than when I do sports at school because those kids are my friends."

"Don't you want to make more friends?" Jake asked.

"I don't like to talk to people I don't know." Jasper looked down. "But the sports stations do look fun. Jake?" He looked up at his brother. "Can you come with me to the club today? You can stay if you want. We can play together."

"Jake, that is a wonderful idea." Ashley smiled. "I don't know why I never thought of that."

"Of course, I would love to go with you, buddy," Jake said. "Are you sure it's fine if I stay with him?" he asked his mother.

"Many of the parents stay with the kids. I haven't been able to because I had stuff to do. This may be what he needs to get out of the shyness," Ashley said.

"Then it's set. Jasper, go get ready and we'll head to the club," Jake said.

"Jake, thank you so much for doing this," Ashley said. "You are the best big brother there is."

"Thanks, Mom. You know I'll do anything I can to help Jasper."

Jasper ran down the stairs a few minutes later with his backpack. "I'm ready!" He excitedly jumped. "Let's go!"

"Jake, the program is two hours long," Ashley informed him. "Why don't you take this to get lunch with him after." She handed Jake extra money. "Have fun, you two."

"Thanks. I'm sure we're going to have fun." Jake smiled.

He drove to the sports club and Jasper practically ran to the front door, Jake trailing behind. "We have to go into the room down the hall." Jasper pointed to the activity room. "That's where the stations are."

"Lead the way," Jake said following his brother down the hall.

"Where is she?" Jasper looked around the room.

"Where's who?" Jake asked.

"The girl mom told you about. She gave me the comic books last week. She said she'd give me more today." He looked around frantically until his eyes spotted Stella. "There she is! You've got to meet her!" He grabbed Jake's hand and rushed over to where Stella was at the polybat station.

"Stella?" Jake's eyes lit up when he saw her.

"Jake!" Stella was surprised to see him with Jasper.

"Wait. How do you two know each other?" Jasper asked.

"We go to school together," Jake said. "So, you're the mysterious girl who gave my brother the comic books he won't stop reading."

"Brother? I had no idea this was your brother," Stella said. She reached down to a bag by her feet and handed them to Jasper. "Here you go, the comic books I promised to give you. Do you want to go and read them?"

"Can we read them later? I want to play polybat with Jake." Jasper smiled.

Stella was shocked to hear Jasper wanted to play polybat, even if it was with Jake and not with her. "Yes, of course, we can. Let me just put them aside so they aren't in the way." She put the bags against the wall and set the polybat station up for them to play.

She watched as the two of them played, the first time she'd seen a smile on Jasper's face since she'd met him two weeks ago. From how the two acted, she could see Jasper was close to Jake. They played for half an hour before Jasper wanted to get into the comics.

"Jasper, do you want me to read the comic books to you like last week?" Stella asked.

Jake was impressed when he saw his brother leave the station and rush to sit next to Stella on the floor. Jake sat opposite them, watching as his brother listened attentively to Stella reading the books. He hadn't seen his brother react this way to anyone new in a long time. On top of everything else, when Jake agreed to come along today, he had no idea he was going to end up spending the morning with his brother and the girl he had a crush on.

"Can we play a game?" Jasper asked Stella.

"Sure. What do you want to play?"

"How about a game the three of us can play?" Jasper suggested.

"Let me see what I can find." Stella got up and went to the cabinet where they kept the board games. She came back a few minutes later with a box. "I found *Happy Hippos*."

"Jake! We love that game!" Jasper said. "We play it every Friday night."

"Do you, now?" Stella smiled and looked at Jake.

"We have Friday nights set aside for a family game night. Jasper's favorite game is *Happy Hippos*."

"Well then, I'm glad we had it here. Are we ready to play?"

The three of them played the game, making sure Jasper won each time. Jake was enjoying himself and Jasper was too.

After five games, Jasper was getting tired of playing the game. Jake knew this would eventually happen, but he was surprised his brother was able to sit still this long with the game. "I want to play at a station," Jasper announced.

"Great!" Stella said. "Where would you like to go?"

Jasper looked at his brother, waiting for him to give an answer. "Jasper, this is your day. You choose what you want to play, and I'll come with you," Jake said.

Jasper looked around and stopped when he saw the archery station. "How about that one?" He pointed.

"That's a very good idea," Stella said. "Do you know that's the most popular station we have here? Even more than the polybat station."

"Really?" Jasper's eyes opened wide. "Come on, Jake! We have to go over there!" He grabbed his brother's hand and rushed to the station.

"Go ahead," Stella told Jake, laughing. "I'm going to put the game away and I'll join you." She walked to the cabinet and put the game away before heading back to the polybat station. She stopped to take mental notes on how Jasper was when Jake was around. Jasper didn't look or act like the same kid she'd seen the past two weeks at the club. Jasper was having fun, even when other kids joined. And he was talkative, especially to Jake. That was when everything started to make sense. The day she met Jake at school, and he called her brave for sticking up for Sam. Jake had an autistic brother, and Stella could imagine how bullied Jasper must've been in the past.

"What's going on?" Jake asked.

"I'm sorry." Stella shook her head. "I guess my mind wandered. What were you saying?"

"I noticed you seemed someplace else." Jake laughed. "All I said was I'm glad Jasper asked me to come with him today. I didn't even know this was where he was going on Saturday mornings."

"I have to tell you, this is the most fun I've seen him having here," Stella said.

"My mom told me about him keeping to himself. That was another reason I came today. I knew if I did, he would get involved with the sports. And as you can see…" Jake pointed to Jasper having fun. "He is."

"It's amazing the difference I see in him," Stella said. "Come, let's go join them in the game."

Jake enjoyed the rest of the morning with Jasper and Stella. He was helping Stella put the equipment away as Jasper stayed off to the side reading the comic books Stella gave him this week. Jake hated this was the way Stella found out he had a brother and now he was going to have to ask her to do something he knew she wouldn't agree to. But what other choice did he have? No one else knew about Jasper.

"Well, that's the last of it," Stella said, cleaning up her

station. "You know, it never fails. Every Saturday I'm sad when the morning ends, even though I know I'll be back next weekend."

"You do seem to enjoy being here." Jake nervously laughed.

"I really do. You know, ever since the incident on the first day of school when Brian bullied Sam, I wanted to learn more about autism. After doing some research at the library, I found a signup sheet to become a volunteer. I didn't think anyone was going to call me, but a week later, here I was." Stella smiled.

Jake let Stella continue talking about how she ended up volunteering at Ability Sports Club, but he found it hard to concentrate. He had to tell her what he'd done, even though he knew it was wrong to hide his brother from his friends for no other reason other than he was different. *She'll understand when I tell her why I did this,* Jake tried to justify his actions.

"Stella, do you need to leave, or do you have time to talk?"

Stella looked at her phone. "Well, I'm in no hurry, but they do need the space to be empty by noon. That's when the club opens to the public."

"Don't worry, it'll be brief. I promised to take Jake out to lunch after and he gets to choose where we're going."

"You're such a great big brother." Stella smiled. "Not many would give up their Saturday morning to spend time with their younger siblings."

You won't think I'm such a great big brother when you hear what I'm about to tell you. Hearing the words in his head made him feel more guilty. "I'm not as great as you make me out to be."

"Are you kidding me? Jake, I saw how much fun you were having with Jasper. And I can tell how much he looks up to you," Stella said.

"Stella, no one at school knows about Jasper," Jake blurted out before Stella could praise him even more than she already was. He didn't even deserve that small amount of praise.

"What do you mean no one..." Stella stopped mid-sentence when she realized what Jake was trying to say. "Are you telling me, you've been hiding Jasper because he's autistic?" Jake looked down at his feet, giving Stella the answer she needed. "But how? How could you do that to him, Jake? Look how much he loves you! And how about the way you thanked me for sticking up for Sam? There isn't much difference between him and your brother. And now you're trying to tell me you're ashamed to have a brother like Jasper?"

"What?" Jake's eyes opened wide. He would never be ashamed of his brother. He was hiding his brother for a whole different reason, mostly to protect Jasper from the harshness of the world.

"Why else would you be hiding Jasper?" Stella crossed her arms.

"You don't understand. I've been to numerous schools because of my father's job. And every time the friends I made met Jasper, they would bully me. I didn't want to go through that again, not when I was actually enjoying the school year."

"So..." Stella tried to comprehend what Jake just told her. "You didn't want anyone to know you had an autistic brother because you were afraid you would get bullied?"

"Not only me but also Jasper. He goes to a special school and has friends there, but when my friends met him, they would tease him whenever they came around. And I didn't want to put him through that again. I wasn't going to hide him forever. I was going to tell all of you when I felt ready."

"I can't believe what I'm hearing." Stella shook her head in disgust. "Are you trying to tell me that not even Henry knows?"

"No." Jake shook his head. "And before you say anything, yes I know he's my best friend. But I also thought the others were my best friends in my old schools and they proved to be otherwise. I wasn't ready to introduce you all to Jasper."

"Guess what, Jake? I have met Jasper, and I think he is the sweetest. If I had a brother like him, I wouldn't be embarrassed by him."

"I get it. I was stupid and never should've kept this secret. But there's something else I need to ask of you."

"What else could you possibly be hiding from me?" Stella didn't know if she was ready to hear anything else coming from Jake's mouth.

"Can you promise me you won't tell anyone about Jasper? I'll tell them when I feel it's the right time."

"Look, you won't have to worry about me telling them. It's not my place to be the one to let them know about Jasper. You should tell them. And the longer you keep it a secret, the more upset they'll be at you. That's how I feel,"

Stella said. "I really have to go," she said, grabbing her purse and rushing out of the building and straight to her car.

Stella sat in her car, angry at Jake. She couldn't believe him and his reason for hiding Jasper. "I should've known!" she said out loud. "He's no different than Brian. How could he say he liked how I stood up for Sam when he was hiding his brother?" Jake said he was hiding Jasper because he was afraid his friends would make fun of his brother, but Stella had a feeling there was more to it. Jake was more worried he would be bullied, not Jasper. He was only thinking about himself and not putting his brother's feelings into account.

After calming down, Stella drove out of the club's parking lot and headed home. She was going to do all that she could to get Jake off her mind. *I can't believe I thought he was different from the other boys in our school.* As angry as she was at him, she was going to keep her promise and not be the one to tell the others about Jasper. She just hoped Jake would come to his senses and tell them sooner rather than later.

Chapter Thirteen

Jake was nervous walking into school Monday morning. He kept replaying the conversation he'd had with Stella in his mind for the rest of the weekend. *I was so stupid for hiding Jasper in the first place.* He never thought of his reason for doing so as being embarrassed by him, but when Stella said that word, he was beginning to wonder if it was true. *Maybe deep down, that is the reason why I was doing this. I never hid him from anyone before, but then again, I didn't have a best friend like Henry at the old schools I attended.* Stella said she wouldn't tell anyone his secret and Jake trusted her to keep the conversation from Saturday a secret. But now, it was up to him. He had to find the perfect time to tell Henry and today, after school when they were painting the sets, was going to be when Jake came clean about his secret.

He was quiet for most of the day, trying to figure out how he was going to bring up the conversation when he met up with Henry later. The day went quicker than usual, and before he knew it, he was standing in front of Mr. Phelps' door. *Best just get it over with.*

Slowly, he turned the doorknob and found Henry already there, beginning to paint the sets. "There you are!" Henry turned when he heard the door open. "I thought you forgot about stopping by today. You're usually here before me." He laughed.

"Sorry, I had to take care of some things," Jake lied. He had no excuse as to why he was late, other than he was trying to avoid this moment. "So, what do we have to do today?"

"All of this." Henry pointed to the boards laying across the floor. "I know we can't get it all done today, but it's a lot. There's so much background scenery for us to paint and not enough time. I don't know how we're going to get this done in time." He started to panic.

"Henry, calm down," Jake said. "As you said, we don't have to get this all done today. Maybe we could start meeting at lunchtime to get extra work in. We don't spend much time eating in the cafeteria anyway."

Henry started to calm down. "You're right. That's a good idea."

Jake grabbed his paintbrush and started to get busy painting. He kept opening his mouth to tell Henry about Jasper, but a sound never came out. *You have to do this. Stella is right. The longer you wait, the worse it'll be.* "Henry? I need to tell you something," he finally spit out.

"Can it wait? We really need to finish at least these five."

"No, this is something that can't wait."

Sensing something was wrong, Henry put his paintbrush down and turned his attention to his best friend. "What's wrong? Don't tell me you asked Stella out, and she turned you down."

"Oh, I wish that was the case. I doubt Stella will be talking to me anytime soon." Jake shook his head.

"Why? What happened?"

"I'll explain that later. Right now, there is something more important I need to tell you." Jake took out his phone and opened the photo album on it. "I never told you, but this is my brother, Jasper."

Henry took Jake's phone and looked at the picture before handing it back to Jake. "You never told me you had a brother."

"I know. And there is a reason why. A stupid reason, but..." Jake was ashamed he did this in the first place. "He has autism. And the reason why I never told you about him was that I was afraid of how you would react to him."

"Wait, let me try and understand this. You have a brother you never told me about because he has autism? Is this the reason why you never wanted me over at your house?"

Jake looked down at the floor and nodded. "You have to understand why I did this."

"Oh, this has got to be good." Henry laughed. "What reason could you possibly have for never telling me you have a brother?" He crossed his arms.

"In the other schools I've been in, they always bullied me and teased Jasper when they found out he was autistic."

"I'm your best friend! How could you think I would act that way towards you if I met Jasper?" Henry was offended. "I can't believe this!"

"Those kids that bullied me, they were also my friends. Or I thought they were." Jake sighed. "Look, I know you and the other guys aren't the same as those kids from my old schools, but I didn't know how you would react if you met Jasper."

"How could you not trust me, Jake? How? I was the first friend you made here when you came to this school, and you really thought I would start to bully you or your brother? This is unbelievable. This is why Stella isn't talking to you, isn't it? She found out."

Jake slowly nodded. "She's volunteering at a sports club Jasper goes to every Saturday. I took him on Saturday and Stella is the only person there he'll go near. She wondered why I never told her about Jasper, and I told her the same thing I told you and she wasn't too happy with me. And then I made her promise not to tell anyone."

"It's no wonder she doesn't want to talk to you." Henry threw his paintbrush on the ground and got up.

"Where are you going?" Jake asked.

"I don't want to be near you. I don't associate with those who are liars and hide things from their best friends."

"What about all the sets we need to paint?" Jake asked.

"I'll continue working on them when you aren't here. I'm going to the auditorium to see if Mr. Phelps needs any help there." Henry walked out of the room, slamming the door.

Jake sat on the floor and leaned against the wall, putting

his head in his hands. *I was so stupid and now I don't have a best friend.*

Great. I blew it. And come tomorrow, he knew the other guys would know what he'd done. *A day is all he needs to be angry at me. I bet everything will be fine tomorrow when I come to school.* Jake knew it was a long shot, but he wasn't going to give up hope. He'd lost Stella, he couldn't lose his friends too.

The next day, Henry avoided Jake throughout the day. Jake tried to reach out and say hi a few times, but Henry ignored him. *Alright, maybe he needs some more time to forgive me.* Mr. Phelps didn't need them to paint today, and Jake hoped this would give him time to talk to Henry. The final bell of the day rang, and Jake went to his locker and saw Henry and the rest of the guys hanging out down the hall.

Jake took a deep breath and walked over to the group, not knowing if Henry told the rest of their friends about the conversation the day before. "Hey, guys," he greeted them.

Henry glared at Jake and turned his back on him. "Bye," he said, walking away and the others following him.

"Please, could you all hear me out?" Jake begged. "I can explain everything."

Henry turned to Jake. "I already told them everything, including your insane reason as to why you hid Jasper. They feel the same way I do, hurt that you didn't trust us. We never gave you a reason to believe we would ever bully you." Jake opened his mouth to say something, but Henry stopped him. "There's nothing you can say that will change how deceived we feel."

Jake ignored Henry. He knew there was nothing he could say that would convince Henry he was right in his actions, but he could try and get through to his other friends. "You guys have to believe me. I was nervous. Here I was, in a new school and I didn't think I would make friends. And then I met you guys, and I was so happy. Believe me, I wanted to introduce all of you to Jasper, but then I remembered when I did with my old friends and that's when they started to bully me."

"I told you yesterday, we aren't your old friends. You should've trusted us!" Henry said. "Let's go," he said to the other boys, and they left the building.

Alone, Jasper walked back to his locker and took out the books he needed to bring home for the night. He slammed the door shut, mad at himself for letting things get out of hand. *I was such a fool.* He sadly headed out to his car. *And what am I going to tell my parents?* He knew his mother was bound to ask why he was staying home this weekend when he'd been going out the past few weeks to hang out with Henry.

Jake arrived home and was greeted by Jasper running up to him. "JAKE!"

"Hey, buddy." Jake forced a smile. "Where's Mum?"

"She is getting some work done in the spare room. Jake, why are you upset?" Jasper asked.

"What makes you think I'm sad?"

"Your smile. It's not your normal smile when you're happy," Jasper said.

"It was a bad day at school."

"Were you bullied again?"

Hearing the concern in his brother's voice made his heart break more. *How could I pretend I didn't have a brother?* "Nothing like that." Jake hugged his brother. "Had a lot on my mind and couldn't concentrate." That wasn't a lie, he did have other things on his mind. Jasper seemed to believe what Jake said and rushed off to his room.

Jake went off in the other direction to his room and threw his backpack on his bed. He wasn't in the mood to do his normal routine after school, starting his homework before dinner. Today, he just wanted to lie in bed and think of all the wrong things he did, to his friends, to Stella, and to his family.

The next morning, Jake woke up and walked downstairs for breakfast. Jasper was already sitting there, eating, looking up from his bowl of cereal when Jake entered the kitchen.

"Are you feeling better than yesterday?" Jasper asked.

"What happened yesterday?" Ashley looked at her son. "Did something happen at school? Are you being bullied again?"

"Mom, calm down. It wasn't anything like that. It was a bad day at school, that's all," Jake said.

"What he means is, it was a typical day for a teenager, right?" Murray asked his son and let out a laugh.

"Yes, that's exactly what it was." Jake laughed, putting an end to the conversation.

"Jake, did you want pancakes for breakfast?" Ashley asked.

Jake grabbed an apple from the fruit bowl on the counter. "Actually, I'm just going to take this and eat it on the way over to school. I want to get there early and see if Mr. Phelps needs any help with the sets. There are still so many scenes that need to be painted. I'll see you later," he said to his parents and brother before heading out to school.

Once he arrived, he headed straight to the drama department. He was surprised when he walked in and saw his other friends painting with Henry. Something was wrong with this picture. His friends never showed an interest in wanting to help out, even when Henry asked if they wanted to join. Jake looked around for Mr. Phelps, hoping for an explanation.

"Oh, Jake. There you are." Mr. Phelps walked over to him.

"I figured you would need me here to help you paint the sets if we want to have them finished in time for the show." Jake smiled.

"Well, as you can see, we now have more help than I could ask for." Mr. Phelps pointed out the other students who were on the floor, painting. "This room is getting quite crowded."

"Mr. Phelps, what are you trying to say?"

"Jake, sorry, we don't need you this morning, as there's no more space. Why don't you come by another time?"

"But..." Jake was about to ask why, all of a sudden, his help no longer needed. He took one glance at Henry and got his answer. Henry must've arrived early so he could talk to Mr. Phelps and tell him about Jake. But why did Mr. Phelps have to take Henry's side before listening to Jake? He wanted to argue with Mr. Phelps's decision, but he knew better than to argue with a teacher. "I understand." He looked down at his feet.

"Jake, before you go, I want to say that I do appreciate the work you have already done. I wish there was more space, so you could help too, but if I have too many students, the sets end up being accidentally damaged. I never thought I'd end up with more students than I need."

"I understand." Jake nodded. *I understand that Henry told you he doesn't feel comfortable with me being here and that's why he got the other guys to come help instead of me*, Jake wanted to yell, but he kept the thoughts to himself. He glared at Henry as he left the drama department and stood in the hall, trying to figure out what to do next.

Jake spent the rest of the morning walking aimlessly around the school until it was time for school to begin. Silently, he cursed himself for thinking everything would've been fine between him and his friends by today. He didn't think Henry could stay mad at him this long, but like everything else he'd thought over the past few weeks, he was wrong.

He made his way towards the auditorium where Stella was on the stage, rehearsing. He stopped at the doors and made sure he was out of sight to watch her sing. The longer he stayed, the more he realized how he had to face the consequences of his actions. *This is all my fault. She's never going to speak to me again, and I can't blame her, but I'm not going to give up. I will do whatever I need to, to make things right again.* And he was going to start this weekend when he brought Jasper to the sports club. He didn't know how he was going to do it, but he would show Stella he was proud of Jasper.

Chapter Fourteen

Jake couldn't wait for the weekend for two reasons. One, Henry and the others were still avoiding him and making it quite obvious they didn't want to be around him. At lunch, they looked in his direction as he sat alone and then walked to another table. It bothered Jake only the first day they did it, but after that, he ignored it. He was more interested in seeing Stella at the sports club on Saturday morning. He needed to win her trust first before trying to gain the trust of his friends again.

"I didn't know you were going to take me again this weekend," Jasper said Saturday morning when Jake was driving him to the Ability Sports Club. "I thought Mom was going to take me."

"She was, but I told her since we had so much fun last weekend, I wanted to come with you again."

"This is because you want to see Stella again, isn't it?" Jasper smiled.

"What? What do you mean?"

"You like her, don't you?"

I really must be obvious. Jake laughed. Even his little brother could tell he had a crush on Stella. "See, this is what I mean," Jasper said. "You're blushing. You were doing the same thing when she was with us."

"You've caught me. Yes, I do like her. But you have to promise me one thing. You can't tell her. Can you keep that secret for me?" Jake asked and Jasper nodded. "Good. She doesn't know and I'm waiting for the right time to tell her."

"I won't tell her, but I bet she already knows." Jasper laughed.

"Remember what I said," Jake reminded Jasper before they walked into the club.

"I won't tell her anything. I promise. Now come on, I want to go inside and see what comics she has for me today," Jasper said running inside and straight for the activity room.

"Wait up." Jake tried to catch up to his brother. When he reached the activity room, he saw Jasper with Stella. She handed him another bag containing comic books.

"Jake! I told you she'd have more for me!" Jasper excitedly showed him the books.

"I was wondering who came here with him when I saw him run in here alone." Stella was friendly towards Jake. She had no other choice. She was a volunteer here and couldn't show she was mad at Jake.

"He ran ahead of me. It took me this long to catch up," Jake laughed.

Stella turned to Jasper. "Do you want me to read the comics to you?"

"Can we do it later? I want to play polybat first."

"Really?" Stella was excited to hear Jasper wanted to play at the polybat station before diving into the comics. "Yes, of course, you can. I have it all set up for us to play."

"If you don't mind, I want to play with my brother." Jasper looked up at Jake and smiled.

"Yes. I totally understand." Stella reminded herself that she couldn't push Jasper into anything he wasn't ready for at the time. Only he knew who he felt comfortable around and if it was Jake he wanted to play with, she wasn't going to stop him. "I'll be right here if you need me."

She watched as Jake and Jasper played, Jake letting his little brother win every time. She had to admit, Jake was making it quite entertaining how he let Jasper win at the very last second. Every loss Jake endured was dramatic, causing Stella to laugh.

"What's so funny?" Jake turned when he heard Stella's laugh.

"Oh, nothing. Just thinking about something," Stella said. She didn't mean for the laugh to be heard. She couldn't give Jake any confidence that she was fine with him hiding Jasper from his friends.

"Jasper, maybe Stella would like to play with you," Jake suggested, surprising Stella.

"I...I..." Stella didn't know how to get out of this without sounding as if she didn't want anything to do with Jake. "I don't know if I can." She looked around to see if there was another station that could use her help. She saw that the archery station was more crowded than usual and could use her help, especially since Jake and Jasper were the only ones at the polybat station. "Actually, I have to go over there to help them out. But you and Jasper can continue to play here." She shook her head and headed to the archery station.

Jake sighed, watching Stella walk off. She couldn't stand being near him, not even with Jasper here, putting an end to his plan of talking to her today. He turned back to Jasper. "Shall we play another game?"

"I think I want to go read the comics Stella gave me." Jasper walked away from the polybat station and over to the bag of books. "Do you know why she walked away?"

"She said she wanted to help with the children doing archery because the line is long." Jake sat down next to his brother as Jasper began to read the comics. He could tell Jasper loved spending Saturday mornings with Stella and unless he made things right, it would be best if he didn't bring Jasper here on Saturdays. As long as he was here, he knew Stella was going to stay away. "Do you want me to read the comics to you?"

Jasper shook his head. "I just like the way Stella reads them to me. But if she's busy, I'll read them on my own."

Jake nodded and leaned against the wall, watching Stella for the rest of the morning. *I have to get her to sit down and listen to me. I'd do anything to get her to be my friend again.*

He brought Jasper back home for lunch, not much in the mood to be out after what happened. His mother was surprised when she saw him return two hours after he left the house. "I thought you were going to take Jasper out for lunch like you did last week," she said.

Jake held up a takeout bag from the local fast-food joint.

"I did drive-thru today." He placed the bags down on the table and took out the meals for him and Jasper.

"Is everything alright, Son?" Murray asked.

Jake shrugged. "Not really. I felt like coming home after being out this morning."

"Are you going to hang out with Henry after lunch?" Ashley asked.

"Not today," Jake said. "I have no plans for today."

"Why don't we go bowling today!" Jasper suggested. "Remember, you said one day when we're all free we can go to the mall for glow-in-the-dark bowling."

"That is a great idea," Ashley said.

Quick! Think of something! Jake's mind screamed. Saturday meant one thing, the students from his school would all be at the mall today and he wasn't ready to run into any of his ex-friends, especially with his family with him. He couldn't take that chance in them finding out what he did.

"I don't think that would be a good idea," Jake said.

"Why not?" Jasper asked.

"Well…" Jake tried to think of something that would get Jasper's mind off bowling. "Aren't you tired from all the fun we had at the club this morning? We played polybat for most of the session."

Jasper thought about it for a moment and smiled. "You're right. Plus, I want to get started reading those books Stella gave me today."

The family continued eating lunch and Jasper rushed to his room with the comic books, leaving Jake alone with his parents. Ashley and Murray looked at each other, wondering who was going to be the first to bring up the one thing they were both thinking. Murray nodded at his wife. "Son, what's going on?"

"What do you mean?"

"This isn't like you on a Saturday afternoon, staying home with us. You're usually going out with Henry and your friends. But you said you have no plans, and you don't want us to go to the mall as a family. Something must be up."

"Nothing is going on. I have a lot of studying to do and I want to spend the rest of the day studying," Jake said. He did have a chemistry test on Monday and hadn't begun studying yet. Today would be the perfect day to get it all done seeing as he didn't have anything else planned.

"Well, if it's studying you'd rather do, then we really can't argue." Ashley laughed. "Maybe we can try for next week to go bowling?"

"Yes, that's a good idea," Jake said, hoping he would have everything settled with Henry and the others by then. "May I be excused? I want to get started with my studying." Jake grabbed his plate and cleaned it before heading to his room.

He closed the door and brought his chemistry book over to his desk. The book sat closed on his desk for a few minutes, Jake tapping his pen on the desktop, his mind on everything but chemistry. *How am I supposed to study for this test when all I can think about is how I wronged my friends?*

Jake spent the rest of his Saturday studying, though he wished he was at the mall with his friends. That was the reason why he did all his studying during the week, so he'd have the weekend free. Once he knew this weekend he wouldn't be doing anything aside from taking Jasper to the sports club, he pushed his studying back. It was better than sitting bored in his room feeling sorry for himself.

Jake continued studying for his test and finished up any homework he'd left until the last minute on Sunday morning, giving him the afternoon free. Staying in his room all weekend was driving him crazy, and he needed to get out. He couldn't think of any place in town to go to where he wouldn't run into any of his former friends, but he didn't care. He told his parents he was heading out to the mall to get some fresh air and would be back in time for dinner. This time, if he did run into Henry or the others, he would be alone. He didn't want his parents or Jasper to find out he was hiding Jasper from his friends.

He parked his car, remembering the first time he came to the mall. It felt like a lifetime ago. He walked by the bowling alley, almost tempted to go inside and play a game by himself to bring back the memory of when he played in the lane next to Stella and Tallulah. *That won't look pathetic at all.* He laughed and continued to walk past the alley. He remembered the promise he'd made to Jasper about taking him here one day. *How could I make that promise to him when I was hiding him from my friends?* The more Jake thought about everything, he realized he was completely at fault for his friends no longer talking to him. *I should've told them the truth about everything from the beginning.* He finally understood why they didn't want to hear his excuses. They were his best friends. He should've trusted them not to treat him or Jasper differently. He should've realized by the way Henry took him in as a friend the first day of school they weren't like the friends at his old schools at all. *I really have to think of a way to get them to talk to me again.* He needed his friends at this time.

Jake was beginning to get hungry and headed over to the food court to grab lunch. There wasn't one place he could go to in this mall that didn't remind him of Stella and the fun they had the day when they'd all hung out. He bought his lunch and was looking for a seat when he heard a familiar voice.

"Tallulah, I'm glad you said yes to coming here with me today," Henry said.

Jake walked past where Henry was sitting with Tallulah and grabbed a free table a few feet away, hoping they didn't see him there. He watched the two as he ate his lunch. Henry's arm was wrapped loosely around Tallulah's shoulders, and he leaned down, whispering something in her ear. He wished he could hear what Henry said to her, but whatever it was, it caused Tallulah to throw her head back, laughing.

What I would give for that to be Stella and me. Jake shook his head. And this could have been him with Stella if he had only been truthful from the beginning. He'd hoped coming to the mall would've helped clear his mind, but he was wrong. Everything he saw reminded him of how he'd blown everything.

Suddenly, he lost his appetite and couldn't stand watching Henry and Tallulah cuddling up a minute longer. He got up from his seat, making sure Henry and Tallulah didn't see him, and threw out his half-eaten lunch. He didn't know what to do now, but he wasn't ready to go home. His parents were happy to see him finally going out this weekend, but there would be questions if he returned home only a couple hours after he left.

Before leaving the food court, he took one last look at his ex-best friend and sighed. He was sitting closer to Tallulah, and the two were now sharing a large soda. *Well, at least I don't have to worry about Stella being at the mall hanging out with Tallulah since it appears she's on a date with Henry.* After yesterday morning, he didn't know if he was ready to see her. She wasn't exactly too thrilled when she saw him arrive at the club with Jasper. The last thing Jake wanted was to run into her at the mall where kids went to forget their troubles.

He walked around the mall, feeling like a complete loner. How else would he feel? He no longer had friends, and he was too ashamed to tell his family why he wasn't hanging out with his friends. *What would they think of me?* Then it hit him. What would Jasper think? Jasper looked up to him as if he was some kind of hero. He was anything but one.

He found a cafe that had empty tables and walked in, grabbing a cup of coffee and finding a seat in the corner. He sighed, sipping his coffee and taking out his phone. His finger was on Stella's number, tempted to text her an apology.

Jake: Stella, I know I'm sorry doesn't mean much, but please understand how sorry I am for what I did. I feel so stupid for hiding Jasper from all of you. I never should've and you were right, I should've told all of you the truth from the beginning. Please, forgive me. The one thing I never want is to lose your friendship.

His finger lingered over the send button before he erased the message and exited out of his texts. She would never answer his text and probably delete it the second she saw his name on her screen.

He looked at his phone and searched through his apps until he found the one he was looking for, a game he played whenever he was bored. This game had become his escape since Henry and the others started to avoid him and it slightly helped him get his mind off his troubles.

Chapter Fifteen

A week was all Jake needed to get all his thoughts collected before he tried again to get attention from his friends. He planned everything out, including finally having his friends meet Jasper. Now, all he could do was hope they would forgive him. He'd learned his lesson and would never lie or keep secrets from his friends again.

Friday afternoon, Jake walked to his locker to grab his books for the second half of the day when he saw Henry at his locker. He took a deep breath and walked over to Henry. "Before you leave, can we please talk?"

Henry slammed his locker. "I don't think we have anything to talk about."

"I think we have plenty to talk about. I get it, you're mad at me. You have every right to be. But you have to hear me out. I learned my lesson. I should've never hidden Jasper from you. I should've told you I had a brother. Guess in the back of my mind I kept thinking back to my old school and how those friends treated me, and I shouldn't have done that. You and the guys never gave me a reason to feel I had to keep my brother a secret. And I'll always regret lying to you. But I am sorry. I hate that I didn't put my family first, and I hate that I lost the only real best friend I had."

"I'm the only best friend you had?" Henry's tone softened.

"You heard how the others used to treat me. They clearly weren't best friends like I thought. But you were different. You never treated me like I was a weirdo because I was the new kid here."

Henry was about to respond when the rest of their group walked over. "Guys…" Henry turned to them. "I think Jasper has learned his lesson and I can tell he really is sorry for what he did. What do you say, shall we let him back into our group?"

The others didn't hesitate in agreeing that Jake should be allowed back in their group. "There you go." Henry smiled. "Welcome back."

"To be honest, we did miss you," Patrick said.

"It wasn't the same, it only being the three of us. And now that Henry has got himself a girlfriend, Patrick and I were left on our own most of the time," David added.

"You got a girlfriend? How long has it been since our little fight?" Jake joked. He didn't want to give it away that he saw Henry at the mall with Tallulah last weekend.

"Well, I wouldn't say it's official yet. But you know…" Henry blushed.

"I can tell Henry wants us to drop the subject," Jake said. "I have an idea. I want to make it up to all of you what I did. Are you guys free this weekend?"

"Considering we aren't the most popular kids in the school, we're free." Henry laughed.

"Why don't you come by my house tomorrow afternoon? I'm sure Jasper would love to meet the rest of my friends. Around two or so. That gives us time to get the house ready after I bring him to the sports club in the morning."

"Sounds good to us. Let's meet after school and make the plans," Henry said.

The boys parted ways to head to class, Jake in the best mood he'd been in for weeks. He meant every word he said in his apology, and he hoped word would get back to Stella. He had a feeling it would, considering Tallulah was now Henry's girlfriend. *Baby steps, Jake,* he reminded himself. As much as he wanted to get Stella back as a friend, he couldn't rush anything. He had to make her see he was sincere with his apologies, not only saying meaningless words to get her back as a friend.

He walked to his English class and took his seat, waiting for the teacher to come in, but he knew it was going to be hard to concentrate. He had his best friends back and tomorrow he would introduce them to his family. Everything was starting to fall into place. All he needed was Stella to be his friend again and then he would take it from there.

Jake didn't take Jasper to the sports club on Saturday. He wanted to get the house ready for when Henry, David, and Patrick came over. Ashley was so happy to hear she was finally going to meet her son's friends; she told him not to worry and she would bring Jasper to the club. As much as Jake wanted to be there, he knew it would be better if he took one week off from going to the club, giving Stella a week of not seeing him. She was still the only one from the group of friends that wasn't speaking to him, but he hoped that would change after this weekend.

Henry and the others showed up at Jake's house at two in the afternoon. "Hey! Welcome," Jake greeted his friends. "Come inside."

"Nice place you have here," Henry said, looking around.

"Who do we have here?" Murray walked into the living room with Ashley.

"Mom. Dad. These are my friends I told you about, Henry, Patrick, and David."

"It's a pleasure to finally meet all of you," Ashley said. "Jake talked about you so much. I'm so glad the four of you were able to finally pick a day to come by. I've been telling him to invite you over."

"Well, they're finally here." Jake laughed, wanting to drop the subject before it slipped out why he'd never invited them over. "Guys, let me introduce you to my brother." He took them to the spare room where Jasper was playing video games on the computer. "Jasper?" Jake knocked on the door to get his brother's attention.

Jasper paused his game and turned to Jake. A smile crossed his face when he saw the other boys with his brother. "Who are they?"

"These are my friends, Henry, Patrick, and David."

"Oh! They're the ones you went bowling with, right?" Jasper turned to the other boys. "Jake told me how fun it was. He said we could all go together, but I don't know when that will be."

"Tell you what. How about next time we plan on going, Jake brings you with him?" Henry suggested. "I mean, if that's alright with you," he said to Jake.

Jake was surprised by Henry's suggestion, but it made it easier for him to bring Jasper with him to the mall now that Henry brought it up. "I love that idea. Jasper is a pretty good bowler. Better than I ever was, I can tell you that."

"Well, then it's settled. We'll pick one weekend, and all go bowling," Henry said.

"Guys, let's go to my room. I have it all set up for us to watch movies. Jasper, feel free to join us when you're done playing your games," Jake said, bringing his friends upstairs to his room.

"Jasper seems like a really cool kid," Henry said when they got to Jake's room.

"Really? I mean, I always thought that, but then again I'm his brother. But, you really do mean it, right?" Jake couldn't believe it. His friends accepted Jasper after meeting him for the first time.

"Are you kidding me? Did you see how good he was playing that video game?" Patrick said. "I wish I had a younger brother as cool as Jasper."

"I have no idea why you were so afraid for us to meet him," David said.

"It does seem stupid now when I think about it," Jake said. "I should've realized you wouldn't be like my old friends. None of them acted this way towards him when I introduced them to Jasper. The second they met him, that was when they turned on me. Now I know you guys would never do that to me."

"You got that right. Now, are we going to stand around and keep talking? Or are we going to watch movies?" Henry took five DVDs out of his backpack. "I brought some in case we couldn't decide what movie to watch."

Jake looked through them and smiled. "These are good choices. And since the three of you are my guests, you can choose which movie to put on. I'm going to go downstairs and get the snacks I bought."

He walked downstairs and grabbed the plates of snacks he'd made earlier and brought them back to his room. Henry already started a movie and Jake put the plates down on his desk. "Feel free to grab some food." He took a seat on his bed and leaned against the headboard, thinking of how grateful he was. Now, all he had to do was get Stella to see how sorry he was and that he would never push Jasper aside again.

Chapter Sixteen

Jake explained to Henry how he wanted nothing more than to get Stella back as a friend. Henry knew how sorry Jake was for the lies he told and agreed to help him. Over the next few weeks, Henry got Tallulah to join in and she passed along the word that Jake finally introduced Jasper to his friends. Stella still avoided Jake in the halls, but he wasn't giving up hope. There had to be something he could do for her to see that he would never lie to any of his friends again.

He skipped out on being the one to bring Jasper to the sports club the past few Saturdays, having a feeling Stella wouldn't want to see him. But after three weeks, enough was enough. By now, she must've known he was hanging out with Henry and the boys again, meaning he saw Tallulah as she and Henry were practically inseparable. His mother was surprised when he offered to take him again, but Jasper was happy. He missed going with Jake. And Jake missed spending Saturday mornings with his brother.

Jake arrived at the sports club, and like last time, Jasper took off into the building, leaving his brother behind. Jake laughed and caught up to his brother, who was already grabbing a new bag of comics from Stella.

"Jake!" Stella was surprised to see him at the club. "I...I didn't think you would be here today."

"Yeah, I've been busy hanging out with the boys on the weekends, but I know Jasper has been wanting me to come back with him. So, here I am." Jake gave a smile.

"Tallulah told me she's been seeing you around when you all go to the mall on the weekends," Stella said.

"Yeah, she's been coming with Henry." Jake hated how awkward the conversation felt. "Stella, I know you still hate what I did, and you have every right. But I want to make it right. I actually came for another reason today."

"You did?" Stella was nervous to hear what his reason was going to be.

"I'm thinking about helping out. If it's alright, I just want to sit back and watch what goes on," Jake said. Once he came clean to his friends, he'd decided to follow in Stella's footsteps and give back to the community and help out.

Stella was surprised by Jake's reason for coming today. She thought he was only here to win her friendship back or ask her out on a date. His words were genuine, and she had to admit, she missed his friendship. "That's a wonderful idea. After, I can speak to Damien and tell him you're interested."

"Great." Jake stood against the wall and watched as Stella read the comic books to Jasper. He didn't last long with the comics, wanting to play polybat.

"Why don't you two play together against me?" Jasper suggested.

"I don't want to get between the two of you," Stella said. "You two look like you have fun when playing against each other." She wasn't sure if she was ready to start being friendly with Jake yet. She looked at Jake and saw a huge smile on his face.

"He's right. We should play against him, though I don't think it'll matter. He'll still beat us." He winked at Stella. She knew exactly what he meant. Together, they could make Jasper still win at polybat.

"As long as you're fine with it," she said to Jasper. "Let's play."

The three of them played polybat all morning. Jake and Stella were acting the way they did when they started to hang out. Despite the friction, they both had lots of fun. He was helping her clean up her station before the program ended and took this moment to discuss everything that was on his mind.

"You were right. It was wrong of me to keep Jasper a secret," he admitted.

Stella nodded. "Do you know what I thought when I first met Jasper? This was a shy kid, but I knew deep down he wanted to open up. I should've realized the resemblance between the two of you. To be honest, the piercing blue eyes and blond hair are a dead giveaway. And from what I've seen when you're here with him, he really looks up to you."

"He does. He always calls me his hero. I try telling him I'm nowhere close to being a hero, but he doesn't want to hear it. Henry and the other guys took him into our group the day they met him. I think he likes that other high school seniors want to be his friends." Jake remembered the day the boys came over to his house. "He really is opening up to others. Look, he's talking to the kids over there." He pointed to Jasper with other boys his age.

"This was what I was hoping to see with him." Stella smiled. She knew that Jake being here played a big part in the change she saw in Jasper. "He's like a different kid than the one who first stepped through those doors a month ago."

"You're the first person outside of our family who was able to get him to open up like this. My parents and I really want to thank you for that." Jake smiled.

"Jake?" Stella looked down at her feet. She couldn't believe she was about to ask Jake this question. She tried to fight her mind out of giving him another chance, but there was something different about him today. And she did miss his friendship. "Are you doing anything tomorrow?" She looked up at him, not knowing what answer to expect.

"No. I didn't make any plans. Why?"

"I was wondering…" Stella stopped. *Am I really going to ask him this? And without asking my parents first?* She got this far and couldn't stop now. "Well, if you aren't doing anything, how would you like to come by my house and meet my parents? I've told them all about Jasper and he's the reason I want to keep coming every Saturday. I'm sure they would love to meet his brother."

"I would love to," Jake said.

Stella wrote down her address on a piece of paper and

handed it to Jake. "Give me a call and let me know what time works for you."

Jake took the paper and placed it in his pocket. "I'll see you tomorrow," he said leaving the club with Jasper and a huge smile on his face. He finally got Stella back as a friend.

"**W**here are you going all dressed up?" Jasper walked into Jake's room Sunday afternoon. "You never dress nicely for the weekends."

"That's because I never had a reason to before." Jake smiled at his brother. "Remember yesterday when I was talking to Stella after we helped her clean up? She asked me if I'd like to go to her house and meet her parents."

"Are you going to ask her to be your girlfriend?"

"Not today." Jake laughed. "I'm only going to meet her parents. She told them all about you and the program at the club and wants me to meet them. That's all." He patted his brother on the back. "I'll see you later."

He arrived at Stella's house and nervously knocked on the door. Stella opened the door and smiled. "Jake, please come in." She took his jacket and hung it up in the closet. "Mom. Dad. This is Jake."

"Jake, it's a pleasure to meet you." James shook his hand.

"Stella told us so much about you and your brother, Jasper," Darlene said. "We've been wondering when we would meet you."

"Thank you for inviting me over," Jake said.

"Let's all go sit in the living room and talk," Stella said. "My brothers are out at a friend's today. Consider yourself lucky. They would never leave you alone." She laughed.

"Stella tells us your family moved here this past summer," James started the conversation.

"My father's job makes us move frequently. But the company told him the move here is the final move he'll have to make. I couldn't ask for a better town to live in. I made so many great friends at school." He looked at Stella.

"Jake is the one who saw me stand up to Brian," Stella pointed out. "He was the first person to say I was brave for doing what I did."

"My brother is autistic, and I've seen him get bullied for that reason many times. I only wish I could've been as brave as Stella to put an end to it," Jake said.

"Jake takes his brother to the sports club every weekend and I'm glad he does. It helped Jasper open up. Now, Jasper plays with the other kids in the program." She turned to Jake. "Remember I told you I was going to speak to Damien after you left about you helping out at the club?"

"Yes." Jake didn't think he had a chance at becoming a volunteer. He'd never met Damien before. All he was to the other volunteers was a brother bringing his younger brother in every Saturday. He hoped Stella would put a good word in for him.

Stella's smile widened. "He said he would love to have you join our volunteer team!"

"Really? When can I start?" Jake was ecstatic.

"Damien said to stop by early next Saturday so he can

show you around," Stella explained. "It's going to be fun working alongside you."

Jake spent the rest of the afternoon having lunch with Stella and her parents. They asked him questions about where he used to live before moving here. And her father made it a point to let Jake know he thought he was nicer than Brian.

He left a few hours later and couldn't wait to get home and tell his parents and Jasper that he was going to start volunteering at the sports club on Saturdays. Jasper was going to be thrilled to hear the news. On top of everything else, this was going to do wonders for his college application. Henry spoke to Mr. Phelps and Jake was back on the production team of the musical. Most importantly, Stella was back to being his friend and now they would be working together every weekend. Things were finally falling back into place and Jake vowed he'd never do anything that would jeopardize it again.

The next weekend, Jake arrived at the sports club early as Stella suggested. She was already there and introduced him to Damien. "Jake, how about I take Jasper with me, and we'll go read some of the comic books I brought in today while Damien shows you around?" Stella said.

Jake looked at his brother and saw the look of excitement on his face. He knew Jasper wanted to get immediately started with the comics and him going off with

Stella would help Jake concentrate on what Damien was saying to him. "Great idea." He smiled. "Jasper, I will be with Damien if you need me," he told his brother and walked over to Damien across the room.

Damien took his time showing Jake all the stations, giving him a little information on each of them. "Now…" He brought Jake back to where Stella was sitting on the floor next to Jasper. "I've put you down to run the polybat station with Stella. I've seen how popular it's become, and she could use help. The kids should be coming in soon, so I'll leave you two alone to get everything set up."

"I knew when I agreed to volunteer here we would be working together, but I didn't expect us to be this close," Jake teased.

"Want to know a secret? I've been hoping Damien was going to have someone join me at the station and I'm glad it was you."

The two of them continued to get the station set up for the kids while Jasper stayed against the wall reading the comic books. "He really does love the books you give him," Jake said once they were ready to start having kids come to their station. "Every night he asks me to come into his room to read them with him."

"I'm glad to see how much he loves them. At least now I know they won't go to waste. My brothers just toss them aside once they finish the books. I'd rather see them go to someone else instead of the garbage," Stella said.

Jake was about to say something when the sound of kids screaming could be heard down the hall. "Guess it's time to get busy." He laughed.

"I have a feeling their time here is the most fun they have all week. I know it's only for two hours, but that's two hours of pure delight for these kids," Stella said. "Get ready. The line for our station is almost as long as the archery station now."

Stella stepped aside to watch Jake play with the kids as the morning continued. Her heart melted when she saw how good he was with the kids, making each of them win. The smile on their faces as they left to go to the next station was all she needed to confirm she'd made the right decision to forgive him.

Jake walked over to her when there was a break in their line. "That's it? We don't have any more kids that want to play?" he asked.

"For now." Stella laughed. "There is a chance some may come back later."

"What do we do now? Just stand there and wait? Damien didn't tell me anything else except that I was at the polybat station with you."

"Usually, I'm staying with Jasper because he stays here with the comics. But if I see a station is crowded and they need help, I'll go over and help."

"Good idea," Jake said. "I think I'll take a walk around and see if anyone needs help. Plus, I'm sure Jasper wants his usual reading time with you." Jake smiled.

He started to walk around the activity room, looking to see if any stations looked as if they could use his help. He didn't know what made him think of this idea, and it wasn't because he wanted to be away from Stella. He loved the idea that they were working at the same station, but he wanted to show her he truly was there to help and not only to be next to her.

As he walked around, he occasionally looked back at Stella sitting on the floor next to Jasper and smiled. The sight was beautiful. His little brother, who was always afraid of talking to strangers, opened so easily to Stella. And from what he could see, Stella adored Jasper.

Chapter Seventeen

The next few months were busy for everyone. Stella was spending most of the week rehearsing for the play after school and spending Saturdays at the sports club. Tallulah was in the orchestra for the musical and spent most of her time with Henry when she wasn't practicing playing the flute. And Jake was with Henry, Patrick, and David finishing painting the sets in time for the production. Now, everything was finished, and they all gathered in the drama room to take a final look at their work before bringing the sets backstage.

"I can't believe it. We actually finished it in time," Henry said. "Did you think it would be possible?"

"I'll admit, I thought we wouldn't get it finished, especially once we lost Tallulah when she had to start rehearsing with the band," Jake said.

"I hated that I had to stop working on the sets, but you four got it done without my help," Tallulah said. "What happened to the other students who were helping?"

"They all quit for one reason or another." Henry shrugged. "We didn't need them anyway."

"Stella, you've been quiet," Jake said once they all made it to the auditorium and placed the sets backstage. "Is everything alright?"

"Fine." Stella shook her head and smiled. "I'm just looking at everything and can't believe everything that's happened. It seems like it was only yesterday I found out I got the role of Sandy and now, the play is in a couple of weeks. And..." She looked up at Jake. "So much has happened since we first met each other."

"And I'm so glad I went up to talk to you that day." Jake smiled. "Guys!" He called the rest of his friends over to where he stood with Stella. "I have an idea. Since we've all been working extra hard to get everything done in time for the play, why don't you all come over to my house tonight? I'll order pizza and we can have a movie night."

"Sounds like a great idea. Count me in," Henry said. The others agreed with Henry, and they all made plans to meet up later that night at Jake's house.

Stella was the first to arrive at Jake's house. She was always early, and Jake was glad to be alone with her before the others arrived. She helped him get the living room set up for movie night and Jake ordered the pizza so it would be there when his friends came over.

"Stella..." He sat next to her on the couch. "I have

something I need to tell you." Jake had this planned all day and now that the time was here, he hoped he could get the words out without being nervous.

"What is it?"

"There's been something on my mind since the day I saw you stick up for Sam in the cafeteria. And then I met you and I knew there was something about you. I couldn't ask you what I wanted back then because you were still with Brian. After you broke up with him, I kept trying to find the right time, but I couldn't find the right time. Until now." He looked down at his hands folded on his lap before looking up into Stella's eyes. "Stella, would you like to be my girlfriend?"

"Jake, I...I don't know what to say." Stella smiled. "I would love to be your girlfriend."

Jake didn't have time to celebrate Stella saying yes to his question when there was a knock on his door. "Guess they're here." He laughed and got up from the couch. He opened the door and welcomed his friends inside. "Perfect timing. Pizza is going to be here soon."

"Great! I'm starved," Henry said and stopped when he saw Stella already sitting on the couch. "What did we miss?"

"Well..." Jake went to sit next to Stella. "I think we should make the announcement together since everyone's here. I asked Stella to be my girlfriend, and she said yes."

They congratulated Jake and Stella, surprised it took Jake this long to ask Stella. The pizza arrived not long after and everyone grabbed a slice and sat around the television.

Jake went up to his room and brought down a few DVDs. "Here are some choices. I have more if you want to watch more than one movie."

The group chose a movie, and Jasper came running down the stairs. "Hey! Did you start the movie?"

"I just put it on. You made it down in time," Jake said. "Pizza is on the table if you want any."

"Jasper!" Henry called him over. "Buddy! I was wondering when you would show up. Sit next to me!"

Jasper grabbed his pizza and sat next to Henry. Out of all Jake's friends, Jasper bonded with Henry over their love for video games. "I'm glad Jake invited you guys to come today." He leaned forward and waved to Stella.

Jake took his seat next to Stella. "Wait until I tell Jasper we're now a couple. He's been asking me every Saturday when I was going to finally ask you out." He laughed.

"Want to tell him now?" Stella asked.

"Trust me, it'll be better to wait. Why don't you stay after everyone leaves later and we can tell him together? He's going to be so excited, it would be best to make sure everyone is gone. Plus, I want to tell my parents too. We'll tell them all at once."

"Good idea." Stella smiled. She tried to concentrate on the movie, but it was hard. She kept thinking back to an hour earlier when Jake asked her to be his girlfriend.

"What's going on in your mind?" Jake asked, noticing Stella wasn't paying attention to the movie.

"Oh." She softly giggled. "I'm thinking about how differently I feel after you asked me to be your girlfriend than when Brian asked me. I'm actually happy this time around. Last summer, I wasn't excited knowing I was Brian's girlfriend. I should've seen that as a warning sign."

"That's all in the past." He put his arm around Stella. From across the room, he saw Jasper look at the two of them with a smile on his face. "You don't need to think about Brian anymore. And if he ever bothers you, you come and get me." He got close to Stella's ear to whisper. "Look at Jasper's face. I think he's sensing something between us. It may be easier than I thought for us to tell him we're a couple."

"He's going to be happy, that's for sure." Stella smiled.

Jake looked around at everyone in the living room. Tallulah was cuddled up to Henry. The two officially became a couple a few weeks ago, though everyone saw it coming. Those two were inseparable when they weren't busy with the play. Even when they had group outings to the mall on the weekends, Tallulah and Henry walked off on their own, meeting up with everyone for lunch.

Patrick and David were the only two single ones in the group, though Patrick had his eyes on one of the girls in the play. He hadn't asked her out yet, but he said he was working up the nerve to ask her once the play was finished. David swore he wasn't looking for a girlfriend and didn't want any kind of relationship until he was in college. His mind was always focused on his studies, and he was working towards a full scholarship for college.

Jake held Stella close, joy overwhelming his heart. He had his mother, his father, his amazing brother, Jasper, and he had Stella, his friends, and their families that had become his family as well. It all rounded up to one thing—love. He had so much love in his life. He was happy; he had found his home, in Ocean Bay, with them. Indeed, home is where the heart is. He looked down at Stella wrapped in his arms and kissed the top of her head.

www.ingramcontent.com/pod-product-compliance
Lightning Source LLC
Chambersburg PA
CBHW040227170726
48295CB00014B/832